THE **TOUCH** OF NATHAN PEERLESS

A novel by
Kevin Wollenweber

"The Touch of Nathan Peerless," by Kevin Wollenweber. ISBN 978-1-63868-213-4 (softcover).

Published 2025 by Virtualbookworm.com Publishing Inc., P.O. Box 9949, College Station, TX 77842, US.

TABLE OF CONTENTS

PROLOGUE

Paul, also known as Saul of Tarsus, Paul the Apostle and Saint Paul, was a Christian Apostle who spread the teachings of Jesus in the first century. For his contributions towards the New Testament, he is generally regarded as one of the most important figures of the Apostolic age.

The main source of information on Paul's life and works is the Acts of the Apostles in the New Testament. Approximately half of its content documents his travels, preaching and miracles. Paul was not one of the Twelve Apostles, and did not know Jesus during his lifetime. According to the Acts, Paul lived as a Pharisee and participated in the persecution of early disciples of Jesus, in the area of Jerusalem, before his conversion.

Paul was traveling on the road to Damascus so that he might find any Christians there and bring them "bound to Jerusalem". At midday, a light brighter than the sun shone around both him and those with him, causing all to fall to the ground, with the risen Christ verbally addressing Paul regarding his persecution in a vision.

His conversion was truly miraculous and in his First Epistle to the Corinthians, chapter 12, Paul wrote to the church in Corinth concerning the spiritual gifts. All the gifts are manifested to each of his believers just as He wills. The gift of healing is referenced in 1 Corinthians12, verse 9;

> "to another faith by the same Spirit,
> to another gifts of healing by that one Spirit,"

The Touch of Nathan Peerless is a fictional tale about a simple man upon whom the gift of healing has been bestowed by the Holy Spirit. This author has been intrigued by the teachings of Paul and my journey to understand my own spiritual gifts has inspired the creation of the characters in this novel.

I have attempted to understand just what a man with the power to heal might experience and the attraction from both good and evil.

May you be blessed by both this story and my Lord and Savior, Jesus Christ, as you read this story.

Kevin Wollenweber

CHAPTER 1
THE PAIN OF GUILT

Sandy Black was suddenly awakened by the birds outside her bedroom window tormenting her with their summer songs and chirping so loud that she couldn't ignore their morning conversation. She grabbed her pillow and used it to cover her ears, hoping to drown out their chatter, but to no avail. Sleep was the only bastion of relief she received from the intense pain that consumed her very existence. If it weren't for pain, she often wondered, would she feel anything at all?

She over medicated herself with prescribed pain killers because taking those extra pills was the only way she could fall asleep. Once she did, and the pain in her body eased, Sandy would dream. Sometimes she dreamed she couldn't wake up. If the pain killers could get her to that point, that point where the pain was absent from her existence, and she could live once again only in her dreams, then this was the reality she desired. Except this morning, those damn birds had other plans for her.

As she struggled to pull and roll her body to her left side to begin the morning ritual of getting out of bed, the pain in her lower back claimed ownership of her body and made her almost faint. It was a piercing pain that felt like somebody

1

had stabbed her lower back with an ice pick. The intense pain was always followed by a burning sensation as though a Fourth of July sparkler had been thrust into her until it eventually expended its fuel. Sandy grimaced and clinched her teeth trying to hold back the scream that was to come. This morning she couldn't hold back the scream enough to keep her mother from hearing it.

Over the last year Angie Black had listened to the frequent cries and screams of her sixteen-year-old daughter more times than she could count. With every moment of pain that her daughter expelled, Angie wished it had been *her* in the car wreck. What mother wouldn't want to take that pain away from a child and onto themselves? Angie did her best to try not to show Sandy the anguish and guilt she felt for letting her daughter leave with friends that fateful evening. She shouldn't have let her go, but she was just trying to allow her to grow up!

Angie rushed into Sandy's room and bent down to help support her legs and back, then assisted her daughter into a sitting position. "Honey, why do you try and do these things on your own?" Angie spoke in a soft, motherly voice.

Sandy, with an irritated expression and all the scorn of a prisoner who was being denied their freedom, replied, "Because I'm supposed to, mother! My therapist told me to start trying to get up and around on my own. If I don't try and move more, I can never hope to get better."

Angie retorted, despite not having faith that her daughter would, or could, ever get better, "Well, I have no doubt you'll be able to do everything on your own very soon, but there's no shame in letting your mommy help!"

Sandy knew her mom loved her dearly, but she also knew her mother would be hard pressed to ever let her go, even if she could, ever again. "Mom, do we own a gun?" Sandy sheepishly asked in a manner that was obviously trying not to draw too much attention to the question.

Angie gasped, not allowing the question to go without angst, and with a scolding response, replied, "Why would you ever ask such a question?"

Sandy let out a bellowing laugh and answered, "Oh, it's not for me. I just want to shoot those damn birds outside my bedroom window!"

Angie was relieved and finally let a small smile pierce her lips. It was very evident that Sandy was suffering from depression. Who wouldn't be, after meeting the front grill of a pickup truck head on from the front passenger seat she was travelling in? Angie worried about questions like the one her daughter had just asked. There were many hours spent worrying that her daughter might want to take her own life. She was always on the alert for signs that Sandy was contemplating permanently ending the constant agony. Angie sensed that the pain pills from Dr. Johnson weren't lasting for as long as they should. As she assisted Sandy, gently easing her into the wheelchair that had also become where she spent all her waking hours, Angie turned towards the bedroom door and spoke to her daughter, "I'll go make your favorite pancakes for breakfast, honey. Remember to take your pills before you come out to the kitchen." Angie thought just how ironic that request might seem to a person that was constantly in pain, and she couldn't help being worried that her daughter might be taking too many of the pain pills anyway.

Angie wanted to display to her daughter that she was going to try and give Sandy some control of her life, so she had made the decision to let her sixteen-year-old daughter manage her own pain and the medication that usually relieved it. It was a decision that Angie often wondered why she had made.

As Angie scooped fresh blueberries into the pancake batter, she watched as a square of butter began to sizzle on the griddle. "I made you fresh squeezed orange juice too, my dear. It's on the table."

Sandy grunted out a "thank you" directed towards her mother. Before she rolled out to join her mother in the kitchen, Sandy caught a glimpse of a teenage girl in her bedroom mirror. Sitting in the wheelchair, she no longer recognized the young girl that existed in the mirror. She envisioned a sixteen-year-old girl with short brown hair and a rounded face with big brown eyes. A girl that was on the verge of womanhood. A girl that was ready to begin her life. A fun life, a popular life, one that other teenage kids would be attracted towards. She was brought back to reality to now see a broken body, with matted hair that had yet to be brushed straight after a fitful night of attempted sleep, in that same mirror. The dark circles under her eyes spoke volumes about the shell of the beautiful girl she used to be. Her face was now thin, almost gaunt. She had seen enough and exited the bedroom.

Rolling her wheelchair up and under the end of the kitchen table, she locked in the wheels and grabbed the juice in her left hand. The pain was not too bad right now, mainly because she had taken another pain pill prematurely. The mail was sitting on the table next to the orange juice, which her mother had so lovingly placed there for her beloved daughter to drink, and Sandy picked up the pile of mail and shuffled through it. "Damn, mom, we have a lot of bills!" Sandy said sarcastically.

Angie caught herself in the middle of her response, "Yes, it seems like we get more medical bills every day." Realizing this comment was not going to be perceived in any other way than accusatory, she looked at her daughter with a look that was begging for forgiveness.

Sandy smiled at her mother and responded, "I know what you meant, mommy. Where are my pancakes?"

Both girls laughed as Angie carried the breakfast plates to the table and set them down. As Sandy lifted her fork to her mouth to take a bite of her mother's special blueberry pancakes, she held in her other hand a postcard that was in the pile of mail. After scanning the text and pictures, she was about to put it back on the kitchen table when something caught her eye. It read: *Are you sick, injured, or crippled, and in need of healing? Come to our service and pray to receive the power of healing through our Lord and Savior, Jesus Christ!*

Angie watched the captivated face of her daughter as she read the large postcard over and over. "What do you have there, sweetheart?" Angie queried.

"I'm not really sure." Sandy replied, as she continued to flip the postcard from front to back.

Hesitant to take a drink, Angie held the coffee cup to her lips. Pausing in deep thought, she was curious as to what her daughter had discovered in the mail. A memory suddenly entered her thoughts, provoking a flashback to the day she gave birth to Sandy. She was the same age as Sandy was now, when she gave birth at only sixteen years old. A mistake, one night, with a boy she had only just met at a school football game. The boy was from a rival high school and was at least a couple years older than her. That boy never knew he had a daughter, and he never would. Angie had no way of letting this boy know he had a child, because no phone numbers were ever exchanged. She barely understood what had happened to her in the back seat of his car. Ten months later, when Sandy was born, she became Angie's entire world. Leaving the memory behind and returning to the moment at hand at the breakfast table, Angie questioned her daughter, "Come on, what does that postcard say, Sandy?"

"It's from Evergreen Evangelical Church, Mother. The pamphlet says that next Sunday they're having a healing service at the church!"

Angie looked at her daughter as she placed the coffee cup back onto the kitchen table. Not wanting to discount her daughter's interest in the postcard, she asked, "Healing service, what in the world is that?"

Angie motioned for Sandy to hand her the postcard so she could see it for herself. Sandy laid it on the kitchen table and pushed it towards her mother. After reading through the text, Angie spoke with sympathetic eyes at Sandy, "Honey, you can't really believe this is anything but a hoax. Nobody truly gets healed by these types of things. It's a con!"

Sandy, in affirmation, replied, "Yes, I don't really believe it either. Heck, I don't even believe in God. The only thing that is odd about this service is what the postcard says about the Bible and what it says about healing." There, under the invitation to join the service at 9:30 am next Sunday, it read: *Healing can come to believers through prayer and with the laying on of hands by those who have received this spiritual gift from God. Not all will be healed at this service. Perhaps nobody will be healed, but we will all gather to pray and trust in our Lord, Jesus Christ, that he will be faithful to His word.*

Sandy looked intently at her mother, who moments ago had finished reading that same passage, and asked, "Why would they say something like that? Why would they suggest that maybe nobody would be healed? What did they mean by that? Isn't that setting themselves up for failure?"

Angie sat and pondered her response and offered as earnest a reply as she could muster, "My best guess is *everybody* will be healed, and the collection plate will be very full because of it."

Sandy placed her hand over the postcard that her mother had tossed back towards her, and responded, "Well then, maybe we should go on Sunday to prove them wrong. I won't be healed, and everybody will see this is a scam. It will be the proof and save everybody a bunch of money."

Angie picked up Sandy's breakfast plate and took it to the kitchen sink. Placing the plate under running water to wash the last remnants of blueberry pancakes down the disposal, she stopped, turned, and looked at her daughter and started to speak. Hesitating, she thought for a moment before answering, "Sandy, my dear love, I have no desire to watch you be humiliated in front of a Church congregation. Most of these people already know you, and they have already offered prayers for you since the accident. Those prayers did no good then, and nothing will change now simply because we attend this service," Angie responded with regrettable frankness.

Sandy turned from the kitchen table and rolled herself towards the living room of their small old mountain farmhouse. Every turn of the wheelchair resulted in creaks being produced from the original pine wood floor. This house was built in the 1930's by Sandy's great grandfather. There were times when Sandy rolled back and forth over the same creaky floorboard just to irritate her mother. She usually had no reason to cause her mother irritation, but she did it none the less. Today was one of those days, and Sandy had found an exceptionally noisy part of the floor. The only difference was, today, Sandy was truly irritated at her mother, and she had a reason.

CHAPTER 2
A WHISPER

After the strained conversation she had with her daughter earlier that morning, the day turned to dusk, and dusk into night. The entire day had been unusually quiet after the dispute over the postcard had caused a rift between her and Sandy. Angie peaked into Sandy's room through the small crack that was always present that enabled her to hear Sandy in case any issues arose during the night. She rejoiced to see Sandy was asleep. Seeing her daughter sleeping brought some comfort to her because it meant her daughter's pain had subsided enough to allow it.

At almost thirty-three years old, Angie would often look in the mirror at herself, as she applied her nightly regimen of moisturizers, and wonder if she was still pretty. Wiping the product from around her eyes, she couldn't help but notice the dark circles that surrounded them. A good night's sleep often evaded her. Angie had always thought she could be pretty once more, if she had time to work at it. It was hard to find time to work on it when you had a sixteen-year-old daughter confined to a wheelchair who lived in constant pain with every waking hour.

Since she had Sandy early in her life, she was still a young woman. Angie had dated, infrequently, prior to the accident, and it seemed she gathered a lot of admirers from the men in Evergreen because of her looks, but none of the men she dated seemed to want a relationship with a woman who had a child. All they were after were drinks and sex.

She had made that mistake several years ago and vowed to never make it again. Sandy was the love and priority of her life and always would be, but she couldn't help but sometimes feel lonely. She had never experienced adult companionship. The type of relationship that brought a deepness of thought and emotion that was shared between two adults. She felt lucky to have come to Evergreen, Colorado, and with the land and house she received from her grandparents, along with a small inheritance, she was able to be a full-time mom to Sandy. She worked odd jobs around town as Sandy grew older and was in school full time, but then the accident happened. She had to become a full-time nurse, caregiver, and constant companion to a crippled child.

As Angie stood in front of the mirror looking at her black hair that was pulled back into a ponytail, she surveyed her five-foot two-inch frame, and wished she could have been at least five inches taller. She was certain that she detected hints of gray on top of her head. Despite the dark circles forming under her eyes from lack of sleep, she still saw glimpses of hope. She laughed to herself as she thought, "Angie, you are one gorgeous woman. If the right man ever comes along, that fancies having the girl next door that looks like death warmed over, you are sure to snag him!"

With that statement, she rubbed moisturizer all over her face and called it a night. As she lay in her bed, close to exhaustion, and with the need for sleep beginning to conquer her this day, Angie listened one last time to hear any cries of pain coming from her daughter. She thought to herself that maybe she had been too harsh and insensitive with Sandy. Maybe Sandy was truly sincere about wanting to go to the healing service at Evergreen Evangelical. It just pained her to know that it would all be in vain. It would be a waste of time and could potentially hurt her daughter even more. Still, tomorrow she would ask Sandy if she really wanted to go to the service and, despite her motherly instincts that it would promote nothing more than disappointment and pain for her daughter, she would take her.

Angie's eyes began to close and as the fatigue of her mind and body began to surrender to sleep, her eyes jolted wide open. She sat up in her bed and, with her head on a spindle, looked around her bedroom. Her heart was beating fast, and she sprang from the bed to walk towards the door. Quietly, she ventured down the hallway. The moon illuminated the hall just enough as to not require her to turn on any lights. Angie came to Sandy's door and peered through the opening only to find her daughter fast asleep.

Convinced that what she had heard just before falling asleep must have been an aberration, Angie gently walked back into her bedroom, slid into bed, and pulled the sheets and comforter up and around her. Her heart was no longer beating fast, and her pulse had returned to normal. What she had heard earlier frightened her, but she was now convinced it must have been exhaustion. Her eyes once again began to close and just as she rolled into dreamland, she heard the same voice call out to her again, clear as day. It whispered to her, "*Nathan.*"

It was a fitful night's sleep for Angie, and it wasn't because of Sandy. Actually, Sandy was quiet for most of the night. Far better than usual that Angie could remember. She fought her motherly instincts head on and let Sandy get herself out of bed and into her wheelchair. Once her daughter had rolled herself out of her bedroom and into the kitchen, Sandy noticed that her mother was unusually quiet.

"Gosh, Mom, you didn't come running to help me this morning. Don't you love me anymore?" Sandy playfully asked. Sandy knew something was up when her mother didn't respond.

Angie was deep in thought and reflection on what had happened to her last night. Realizing that Sandy had said something to her, Angie regained her focus on her daughter.

"I'm sorry, dear, you asked me something?"

"Never mind, mother. I can see I'm no longer the focus of your life," Sandy exclaimed with some sarcasm in her voice.

Angie walked over to her daughter and bent down to give her a hearty embrace. "Of course you are, my love. My thoughts were just, let's say, preoccupied."

"About what?" Sandy quizzed.

Angie took a moment to respond and when she did it was with a question of her own. "Sweetheart, do you know anybody with the name Nathan?"

Sandy pondered her mother's question. After thinking about it for a few moments, she responded, "Not that I can think of, why?" Then it came to her, "Well, there is a Nathan Peerless who lives in a cabin down County Road 29."

Angie, once again, let her thoughts travel away from the conversation. When they returned to what her daughter had answered, she probed further. "Do you know anything about him?"

"Not much, mom. Why?" Sandy quizzed with earnest curiosity.

"No reason. I heard somebody mention his name. I was just curious who he is."

Sandy could see her mother was still intrigued by who Nathan is. "The only thing I know about him is all my friends from school would see him in town every now and then. They all thought he was sorta cute. Ya know, for an older guy. The only thing we knew about him is he was some kind of religious freak."

"Religious freak? What do you mean by that?" Angie prodded.

"I don't know. I mean, I think he travels around and *heals* people who are sick. You know, religious freak."

Angie went to the kitchen trash can and fetched the slightly greasy, stained postcard that she and her daughter had argued over yesterday. "I've decided we should go to this service at Evergreen Evangelical, just like you wanted."

"It's up to you. Whatever, mom," Sandy sarcastically answered.

CHAPTER 3
THE DUST

Three Months Later

A cool breeze was blowing, reminiscent of the cold air that came from vintage red metal ice boxes that dispensed Coca-Cola bottles. Fall was here, and soon the aspen leaves would lose their grip on their summer branches and begin falling to the ground with hues of yellow, red, orange, and gold. Nathan Peerless had never seen the fall splendor of the New England landscape. He only knew about God's handiwork in his home state of Colorado. He had known people that had visited the east coast, who would talk about the beauty of the fall season in New England, but he doubted it was anywhere near as beautiful as it was here, in the Colorado mountains.

Fall had always been his favorite season. He felt it embodied the whole package. First life, as summer drew to a close, then the slow, colorful transition to the death of winter. Both offered beauty in their own unique way. In his eyes, he knew this was probably the reason he had been born in Colorado. It felt closer to Heaven for him, thus, Evergreen, Colorado, he deduced, had to be closer to God.

Nathan's dog, Jasper, nudged his nose up under the hand of his master. Jasper was a mutt in every sense of the word. It was hard to tell what breed he might be, and Nate suspected he probably had some retriever in him. "For a dog that loves water as much as this dog, he has to have retriever in him," Nate would often think. As he scratched behind the soft cartilage of Jasper's right ear, he looked out onto the clear blue sky that, along with the pine and aspen trees, framed the landscape that led up to the log cabin that was his home. The cabin was modest in every sense of the word. Pine logs in rows, surrounded by mortar to protect the inside from the harsh Colorado winters, were prevalent on the main structure. Upright wood pillars forged the supports that held the roof that overhung and extended out across a porch that ran the entire width of the front of the cabin. It was a simple cabin, just like the type of man he was.

Nate looked down at the worn denim jeans that showed slight rips forming at the knees. New clothes weren't high on the list of things he needed. What he needed was to rest, and he also needed to forget. He believed that he had finally found some of that peace he needed, here at his home in Evergreen. God had worked a miracle in his life. One he so desperately needed. Now his life would never be the same. Peace had come to his soul by the grace of God. Suddenly, a deep sigh extended from his diaphragm. The bellowing that came forth could almost be mistaken for the sound of anxiety. His eyes fixed on the dust that cascaded upward towards the sky from about a half mile down, on the long gravel driveway that led directly to his cabin.

Nathan knew that the dust being kicked up was created by a large vehicle. He didn't really care what type of vehicle it was, and Jasper's black ears stood erect and at attention. The dog knew somebody was coming, and he sensed that his master was suddenly tense. Nate, as most of his friends called him, removed his boot from the support post where it had been perched and stood up from the old rocking chair that adorned his porch. He needed an end to days like this invading his existence. He was tired and didn't want to face scrutiny from anybody, especially the media, any longer. He needed to be free from the corruption that had pursued him for the past year, and he wanted to be free from all the demons from hell that accompanied those that delivered that corruption. As the black Dodge Durango SUV with dark tinted windows came to a stop in the driveway in front of his cabin's porch, Nate, in anticipation of just who these passengers were, mumbled to Jasper, "Yep, just as I suspected, boy. Demons from hell, for sure."

Two figures emerged from the SUV as the dust settled back onto the gravel driveway from which it came. One figure was male, and the other female. Jasper was not a good watchdog, but even if he were, it was clear that he knew both these people. His tail wagged ever so slightly, but he did not leave Nate's side until the female with the slender frame and long silky shoulder length brunette hair emerged from the passenger side of the SUV, lifted her sunglasses and placed them on top of her head. She patted her left thigh with an open hand and beckoned Jasper to come join her. The dog reacted, but just as he reached the top step that descended to where the woman was standing, he stopped to look back at his master. Before proceeding to the driveway below, he sought to gain Nate's approval. "Go ahead, boy. I know you want to go to her and solicit more ear scratching," Nate proclaimed as if the dog could suddenly understand English.

Looking up and onto the porch where Nate was now standing, she called out to him, "Well, aren't you going to ask me up to join you for some iced tea? That is what you're drinking, isn't it, Nathan?"

Nate gulped down the last of the liquid from the glass, and answered the woman with a cursory reply, "I'm all out of tea, Robin. That was the last of it, but you're welcome to come suck on the ice cubes. I don't want you to accuse me of being inhospitable."

Well educated at Rhodes College with a PHD in Religious Studies, Robin Gunderson looked and acted like a sophisticated woman with every inch of her persona. She was extremely well dressed and attractive, but Nate never felt she needed to wear as much makeup as she did. At five foot seven, with deep brown eyes that could freeze anybody like a deer in the headlights, she was, by all standards, a *looker*. This was the type of woman that deplored a simple no frills living with every fiber of her being. This cabin environment was beneath her, and her mannerisms showed it. She climbed the five steps that led up and onto the rustic porch. With wide open eyes showing the seductiveness of their deep brown color, she walked over and stood directly in front of Nate, staring directly into his eyes. Never removing her focus from his eyes, she grabbed the glass from his hand. Robin tilted the glass just enough to bring an ice cube past her lips and into her mouth. Her lips were adorned with bright red lipstick, and she crushed the ice cube she had extracted from the glass with all the precision of a fierce predator crunching the bones of its prey.

Nate's gaze parted from Robin's brown eyes and out to the bottom of the porch steps. Standing at the base of the steps was a tall muscular man with a shaved head and nicely pressed Levi jeans with a red polo shirt of expensive origin. Nate motioned to the red shirted man and called out to him, "You might as well come on up here too, David. Since *I* have Jasper, it's only fair that I let Robin have *her* dog on the porch too!"

Nate Peerless took his right hand and used it to stroke back his full head of salt and pepper hair, which made him look slightly older than his actual age of forty-one years. As his hand slid down the back of his head, he was certain he could feel the hair on his neck standing up.

At six feet two inches tall, he towered over Robin. He had never been considered to have a muscular build, but nobody had ever called him scrawny either. His features were anchored by a piercing smile. The kind of smile that would make strangers believe that he knew them and everything about them. This ability to make people feel safe, especially strangers, was a gift he had discovered when he was a teenager. He often wondered whether this connection was a blessing or a curse.

Despite the times when he questioned this gift, and the power it possessed, he understood that it made people feel comfortable with him. Comfortable enough to let him lay his hands on them and make them feel something nobody else had ever made them feel. His *touch* could reach deep into their souls!

CHAPTER 4
INQUISITION

Nate motioned for David to sit down and pointed towards a pine deck chair on the porch. Reluctantly, David complied, never taking his eyes, which were concealed beneath the dark mirrored sunglasses, off Nate. "Sorry, David, I didn't really intend to infer you were a dog. It was very rude of me, considering Jasper could hear what I said, and he takes being a dog very seriously," Nate smirked with a sense of sarcasm in his voice.

David glanced over at Robin and replied to Nate's words, "I'm here at Robin's request, *healer boy*. Robin's concerned about your mental state and doesn't know what you might be capable of."

Nate always had a pet peeve about talking to people with sunglasses. He liked to read people's eyes. Turning his attention away from David and back to Robin, who had already made herself comfortable in one of the other deck chairs, Nate sat down in his favorite rocking chair. Leaning forward, with his elbows on his knees, he addressed his guests. "So, what can I possibly do for you fine folks today? Or did you just decide that a visit to see good old Nate Peerless in Evergreen, Colorado, would be a great thing to do today?" he asked with the full expectation that his guests would realize they weren't welcome by the tone he exhibited.

Robin, feeling the need to take over as the spokesperson for the visitors, responded in a matter-of-fact tone, "You know why we're here, Nate. Word on the street is that you're performing again and some gal here in Evergreen no longer needs a wheelchair to get around. This makes us believe that you might have *new* handlers. Could any of these rumors be true? Could they be, Nate?"

David, feeling the need, chimed in and handed a postcard to Nate. "Because if this were true, it would be in direct conflict with our agreement. Not only with our agreement, but also the agreement with the State of Tennessee!"

Nate looked gingerly at the postcard and appeared to completely ignore it and its contents. Looking directly at Robin, he answered, "*Performing*. Is that what you call it, Robin? Just a performance for my audience?" Jasper, the dog, wasn't particularly enjoying the tone of the conversation, which prompted him to leave Robin's side and settle in on the porch lying next to Nathan.

Setting the postcard on a small table next to his rocking chair, Nate leaned forward and pushed himself up. As he stood, he grabbed a handful of nuts from a bowl next to the postcard and carefully pushed a few of them into his mouth. Pivoting and walking towards the screen door that served as the entry into the cabin, he stopped and grabbed the empty glass from Robin's hand. With all the strained courtesy he could manage, he said, "I'm going in to get some more iced tea".

Robin was puzzled by his proclamation, "I thought you said you were out of iced tea?"

Nathan, with no expression on his face, quipped, "I am." The dog followed him through the screen door and into the cabin, and both Nate and Jasper disappeared from view.

CHAPTER 5
REVELATIONS

As Robin sat on Nathan's porch dumbfounded about his departure into the cabin, she stared at David with a look of scorn that made him cringe. Almost afraid to speak, he mustered the courage and sheepishly asked the question, "Do you think he's coming back out here?"

Robin slid her sunglasses back on to cover her inflamed eyes. She stood up from her porch chair and, in a matter-of-fact way, answered, "Nope, I think we're done here!" She walked towards the porch steps and took one last glance back towards the door where Nathan had entered the cabin. Part of her secretly wished he had returned and was standing there. She felt guilty for where things were today between them, although she would never let it show. Nobody could ever know that she still cared deeply for Nathan and felt a twinge of responsibility for everything that had happened. She wanted him to come back out onto the porch, take her in his arms and tell her he still had feelings for her. Maybe, just maybe, things would be different this time, if only it were just him and her, nobody else. But this was not going to happen, and she knew it.

Robin's thoughts took her back to the first time she had met Nathan Peerless. As a graduate student, her doctorate thesis was on the *spiritual gifts of God*. She chose this subject because she wanted to tackle the very gift she struggled with the most to believe in, and that was spiritual healing. Her beliefs truly never led to faith that *any* of the spiritual gifts were truly from an omnipotent God. She had read online about a spiritual healer of uncanny abilities that appeared to have a success rate that would validate that he was either legitimate or a very convincing fraud. She suspected fraud. Robin Gundersen believed *everything* about religion was fraudulent and this particular fraud was none other than the man, Nathan Peerless. She got lucky because he was scheduled to be in town at a revival at a church near her residence at Rhodes College. It would be fun to watch this fake at work and expose all the tricks of the trade this con artist possessed.

The outside of the Living Waters Tabernacle in Memphis, Tennessee, was adorned with beautiful oak trees. The grounds were large and nicely groomed. As Robin stepped off the bus that dropped people off for the revival, she was amazed to see a large tent erected on the south side of the church building. This event had the appearance of an old-time country revival and the reason the church had decided to pitch a tent instead of holding it inside the church became evident due to the size of the crowd that was forming.

"How could this many people get duped into believing this crap?" she thought. "There must be two thousand people here, waiting to get into the tent." It looked like a gamble whether those people at the back of the line would even get in, but Robin pushed forward with her attempt to get a seat. It was puzzling to her that none of the ushers at the door were screening the guests, so it was obvious that Peerless wasn't using the old microphone in the ear trick to identify any pre-screened attendees for their ailments and illnesses.

The ushers were simply moving the crowd along to get as many people seated as possible so the services could begin. "Odd", Robin thought to herself, "I guess he'll draw from those people in the crowd in wheelchairs or with crutches." That seemed to be so lame to her. So easy to debunk because those people would obviously be *planted* and placed there with fake injuries. Healed through a miracle provided via this *magic man*. "How very lame", she thought.

Then the service started. Without the fanfare that was usual for a rock star of Nathan Peerless' stature, the choir and band from Living Waters played and sang several spiritual songs. It was upbeat and joyous in nature. Pastor Wayne Edmonds, the lead Pastor at Living Waters, spoke to the congregation that Robin estimated was now at about three thousand people. She had heard it all before. Then Pastor Edmonds introduced the *star* of the show, Nathan Peerless.

As he walked out onto the stage she gasped. *His smile. My God, his smile*. Robin knew deep down that he wasn't looking directly at her, but it sure felt like he was. She was in the back row so how could he possibly see her? She guessed this man at an age of about thirty-five or so and he seemed to be looking directly at *her*! Mesmerized by this, she soon snapped back to reality as he began to speak!

Then this captivating man on the stage of the revival tent loudly proclaimed, "Hello, brothers and sisters in Christ! I come here before you tonight for one reason and one reason only."

Nathan went on to preach to the crowd that his *only* reason to appear before them was so he could pray with all who were believers in the resurrected God, who is our Savior Jesus Christ, and for those attending that did not know Christ as their personal savior, that they would come to accept him tonight! He spoke of the life, death, and resurrection of the Lord, and invited all who did not know him before tonight, but came here to get to know him tonight, to please come forward and the staff would pray with them and give them guidance on where to go from here.

With that, Nathan Peerless ended the service, telling the crowd, wheelchairs, crutches and all, to be safe going home and with that the event ended. Just like that!

Robin sat in a back row stupefied about what she had just witnessed. Where was the con? Nathan Peerless had not even asked for an offering. No money. People began to file out and head to their various homes as Robin couldn't take her eyes off Nathan. He stepped down from the stage and she saw him being introduced to another man that she recognized. The man with whom Nathan Peerless was shaking hands in greeting was a fellow graduate student that she knew. His name was Jim Hobart. He was blind. She knew this to be absolutely true. Jim had been blind since he was six years old due to measles. Robin knew Jim very well from Rhodes College.

She saw Jim Hobart get down on his knees and Nathan Peerless joined him. Nathan prayed with Jim and after a short time he touched Jim on the nose with his right index finger. She could tell they were praying *together*.

A kindly man in what Robin referred to as a *funeral suit* came up beside her. He sat down and spoke to her, interrupting her and distracting her from watching Nathan and her friend, Jim. "Did you enjoy the revival services, miss?" he asked.

Robin, distracted, responded "Yes, very much. I was very much surprised."

"Hmm, how were you surprised?" the older man asked.

"Just, uhm, not what I expected," Robin answered in a less than polite manner. Irritated at being distracted, Robin looked back towards where Nathan and the blind man had been kneeling together in prayer. Nathan was suddenly gone and the people surrounding the blind man were weeping and hugging him. It appeared to her that many of the people surrounding Jim looked pale and upset. "Hmm," she thought, "so much for being a healer!"

Having seen enough disappointment for the evening, Robin got up from her seat, went to excuse herself from the gentleman seated next to her, but he was gone. She hadn't seen him leave, but she guessed her being preoccupied with the event unfolding at the stage had caused her not to notice and she hurried to catch the last bus home.

Despite feeling like none of her questions had been answered, she still couldn't get the piercing smile of Nathan Peerless out of her mind.

There was a quiet place on campus and Robin loved to grab a coffee at the local convenience store and sit there on a bench and enjoy the cool, crispness of the morning. She sipped her coffee before going to the computer lab to work on her thesis. She was excited this morning because this was the day of the week that Jim Hobart usually came to work in the same lab as her. This grassy area was how Robin had come to meet Jim. She couldn't wait to get his perspective on what he thought of the revival last night, and his opinion of the infamous *Nathan Peerless*.

Time seemed to go by quickly that morning and Robin couldn't wait any longer for Jim to stroll by with his usual escort, an undergrad student from Norway by the name of Liesel Jensen. Just as Robin Gunderson picked herself up from the park bench to begin her walk to the lab, she spotted Liesel. She was alone.

Calling out to Liesel, Robin asked, "Hey, Liesel, no Jim this morning?"

Liesel replied "Excuse me. I'm sorry, you said something?"

"I just wondered if Jim was alright this morning. He isn't with you?" Robin inquired.

Liesel just smiled and then she stopped.

"You did not hear the news?" Liesel surprisingly asked.

"No, what news, Liesel?" Robin voiced concern.

Liesel continued, "Jim is no longer blind. He was healed last night, by God!"

Robin felt like she had been sucker punched and let out a gasp. Liesel came over to check on Robin's welfare and asked, "Are you okay?"

"I'm really not sure" Robin choked.

Robin's focus returned from daydreaming about her first experiences with Nate Peerless to the current time on Nathan's cabin porch. Those memories were special to her. They were, she struggled for the right word, *divine*. She felt she had witnessed the true presence of God during that time. How she got pulled so far away from that, she wished she understood.

Robin prepared to exit Nathan's porch along with David Greene, when the glimpse of a figure caught her eye at the same cabin doorway through which Nathan had disappeared.

It definitely wasn't Nathan. The shadow was much too short to be him. The figure stood in the doorway and the wire mesh screen obstructed enough not to reveal itself clearly, perhaps wanting to be noticed but not yet exposed. In a very cautious manner, Robin turned towards the screened doorway.

"Hello there," she said in a puzzled sounding voice. "My name is Robin Gundersen. I came to see Nathan; may I ask who you are?" Robin quizzed.

From the creaking sound of the screen door, the figure emerged to be exposed in the light of day. Robin could see that it was a pretty young woman, perhaps in her thirties, with that *girl next door* look. She answered in a quiet tone. "Hi, my name is Angie."

The passengers from the Dodge Durango both stood facing the mystery woman. There was slight confusion on Robin's face, in addition to surprise. She stumbled for words when she addressed her, "Hel-uhm-hi, Angie. As I said, my name is Robin and this is my friend, David."

"Nice to meet you, Robin and David," Angie offered back in greeting.

"Nice to meet you too, Angie," Robin responded with all courtesy. Robin stated in the politest manner she could muster, "We're so sorry to bother you. We're old friends of Nathan and decided to stop and see him today. We weren't aware he was entertaining a guest."

"Guests," Angie corrected Robin. "There are two of us here with David".

"Oh, now I really feel stupid," replied Robin. In a playful manner that David was clearly unaccustomed to, she slapped his arm and joked, "Did you know Nathan had guests, David?"

"Golly no, I didn't," David said with a forced half joking reply.

"It's me and my daughter. Her name is Sandy," Angie replied.

"Oh, how nice. Are you enjoying your visit to Evergreen?" Robin asked in a tone that seemed slightly ingenuine but was obviously an attempt to further interrogate.

"We live here in Evergreen," Angie answered in a manner that had a hint of disdain for the question.

Robin had rarely been put into a position where she wasn't in control. This was one of those rare moments. The appearance of this woman at the cabin caused her to have a tinge of jealousy. It wasn't long ago that she and Nathan had been together. Truth be known, this woman was just Nathan's type. Simple and natural. Everything she wasn't and could never be.

What was most disconcerting to her was the short amount of time she and Nathan had been apart. This woman couldn't be a romantic interest for Nathan, could she? Robin felt compelled to quiz Angie with her next question. "And so how do you and your daughter know Nathan? Are you friends or neighbors?"

At this moment Nathan Peerless reappeared from inside the screen door along with Jasper the dog, plus a young girl standing directly behind him. He motioned for Sandy to come to his side and placed his arm across Angie's shoulders.

Robin cringed at the sight as Jasper came to the side of this woman that Robin feared had replaced her.

CHAPTER 6
THE TOUCH

Two years ago

As he sat sipping coffee on the veranda of his hotel room, Nathan enjoyed the brisk morning air of Nashville. He had ordered a blueberry muffin to enjoy with his coffee. A light breakfast was usually his meal of choice in the mornings. The aroma of the blueberries was quite prominent and that told Nathan that they were most likely fresh when they were selected to accompany the muffin on its journey to deliciousness.

As he broke a section off and prepared to eat it, the smell reminded him of the blueberry jam his grandmother used to make. As the first bite entered his mouth, his hotel room phone began to ring with the lights at the bottom of the receiver flashing in unison. Nathan stood up from the white wire mesh deck chair and briskly walked into the room to answer the call.

On the other end of the phone line was Pastor Edmonds of Living Water Tabernacle. Wayne Edmonds had called Nathan to advise him that a young woman by the name of Robin Gundersen, who had been to the revival the previous night, was desperate to interview Nathan for her doctorate thesis on the spiritual gifts.

Nathan thought to himself "desperate, hmm?" He told Wayne, "Well, if she's that desperate, then I better meet with her! How about at 2:00 PM?"

Later that afternoon Nathan was sitting in the leather chair directly in front of Wayne Edmonds desk. Rubbing his palm on the smooth, soft leather, he marveled in the coolness to the touch. When the attractive woman with seductive brown eyes was escorted into the office, Robin immediately introduced herself to Wayne Edmonds and thanked him for setting up the meeting. Turning towards Nathan Peerless, who had jumped to his feet by this time, she shook Nathan's hand like she would never let it go. Nathan remembered her. He had seen her in the back of the revival tent the previous night.

"Hello, my name is Robin Gundersen, Mr. Peerless. It is such a pleasure to meet you," She blushed.

Nathan responded in mutual admiration "Just call me Nate, Ms. Gundersen."

"Then, please, call me Robin," she blushed as she replied.

Pastor Edmonds excused himself from the meeting. He guessed there was no reason for him to be present for a question-and-answer session, plus he sensed the flirtatious element of their exchange. After he left, an awkwardness in the conversation between Nate and Robin set in. Nate thought to himself, "She has beautiful eyes." They captivated him so much that he imagined that if he could sit and talk with an angel, it would have eyes just like Robin Gundersen's.

Robin finally broke the awkwardness and said with all frankness, "Nate, I must admit to you that I came to the revival last night on the premise that you were a fraud! I don't believe in healing," she continued, "I don't believe men can lay hands on people and heal their injuries, their sickness, or their *defects!*"

She studied Nathan's smile. My God, what a smile. She also could see he wasn't quick to respond to her statements with anger or defensive outbursts. Robin then turned her angel eyes to look directly into Nathan's and spoke, "Did you heal my friend, Jim Hobart?"

Nate Peerless continued to smile at Robin Gundersen because he couldn't help himself from peering further into her eyes and wondering if, and when, he might get to see her again once this meeting had ended. He felt selfish that the focus of his thoughts was purely on his own desires. He snapped out of it knowing that she sought answers to her questions. Many had questions and needed them answered, Robin Gundersen was no different, despite being beautiful.

Nathan tilted his body towards Robin. It was meant to show complete attention to her question. Instead of answering her question directly, he led with one of his own. "Do you believe I healed him, your friend?" Nate inquired in a manner that set Robin back.

Robin answered in a very unsure way, "I don't know. All I know is he once was blind, but now he sees." Nathan chuckled at this reply from his beautiful interviewer.

"Yes, Robin, he once was blind, but now he sees. But I am not the one who healed him," Nate responded as the smile left his face.

"Ah-ha" she thought to herself. "Now the truth will come out that he didn't heal Jim Hobart." The truth to this fraud will be exposed and she can go back to being a non-believer. She couldn't help but notice how the tone of their conversation had now changed since his smile had disappeared from his face.

"You see, Robin, your friend, Jim, healed *himself*. Through faith and prayer that *his* Lord, Jesus Christ, was capable of healing him! I was simply present with him at the time. I also believed he could be healed. God instructed me to pray and touch him. Jesus does the rest!" Nathan spoke softly, but boldly.

"But how? Just how does God, you know, tell you?" She dropped her gaze from Nate's face and bent her head down towards the ground. Robin began to rub her temples. She rarely had headaches, but she was certain she was getting one at this moment.

"I still don't understand," Robin replied as she rubbed her left temple.

"Do you have a headache, Ms. Gundersen?" Nate inquired.

Just as she was about to admonish Nathan for calling her Ms. Gunderson, she felt a thumb and an index finger on her left temple. The touch was that of a man, except it didn't feel like a man's touch.

Robin felt a cool sensation with that touch, but at the same time warmth, like a blanket fresh from the clothes dryer on a chilly day. She was transported to a place that she didn't recognize. This place seemed like peace, and very much like love.

"Please, call me Robin", she said as she was hurled back to reality. Her focus was regained as she watched Nathan's hand retract from her temple. She gazed at Nathan in a way she had never looked at a man before.

A smile had returned to Nathan's lips as he replied to her request, "Is your headache gone, Robin?"

What had just happened to her was beyond her comprehension. It was like nothing she had ever experienced before. Robin found it difficult to speak, but in her mind she had so much to say. So many questions needed to be asked and more importantly, answered.

Wayne Edmonds had returned to his office to check up on how the interview was proceeding. It became evident to him by the blank stare on her face that something miraculous had happened, and that she was the recipient.

Robin knew it was time to end the interview. Her mind darted and raced to concepts and ideas she didn't even know existed. She shook both her host's hands as she prepared to depart. There was a reluctance to shake Nathan's hand in fear that it might evoke the same sensations that she had just experienced at his touch, but she didn't want to seem ungrateful that he agreed to let her interview him. As she departed, her eyes met Nathan's. It was at this moment that she knew this would not be the last time she saw him.

Days turned into weeks, weeks into months. Robin finished her thesis on the spiritual gifts and received her doctorate from Rhodes College. Her thesis had taken a completely different turn from what she had started or planned. The theme of her final thesis was on the validation of spiritual healing through prayer and the laying on of hands. She owed this revelation to Nathan Peerless. She, herself, had witnessed the healing power of God.

As Nathan Peerless Ministries continued to flourish and his notoriety spread, so did the demand for his appearances. Churches and revivals across the United States were calling and writing, asking for Nathan to come, speak, and most importantly, heal. The bottom line was, he knew they wanted him to come and perform the healing. Robin had left the sanctuary of her school apartment after getting her doctorate and embarked on the next chapter in her life. She accepted an offer to work for Nathan Peerless Ministries.

Robin was falling in love with Nathan, and she couldn't bear to be apart from him as he traveled, so she did the only thing her heart could tell her to do, and that was to beg him for a job. Nathan accepted her into his organization because he was also falling for her.

It was a beautiful fall night shortly before Nathan was to embark on a tour of churches in South Dakota, Montana, Arizona, and New Mexico before ending back in his beloved state of Colorado. Nathan missed his home, and he got excited just thinking that when he finally arrived at his home in Evergreen, the aspen trees would be dropping their leaves in anticipation of winter.

On this night, Nathan and Robin ate dinner together on the patio of a local bistro in Kalamazoo, Michigan. It was hard for them to find time to spend with each other. So many people desired the *touch* of Nathan Peerless, and Robin knew she was sharing him with the world.

"Is it too cold for you out here, Robin? I can see if they can light the gas heater or we can even go inside to finish dinner," Nathan asked.

Robin smiled and responded to Nathan, "Maybe you could just move around to my side of the table and we could snuggle."

Both laughed, but Nathan eagerly obliged.

They sat and shared the battles of each of their days with each other. Robin had taken over as the *Administrative Assistant to Mr. Peerless.* This is how she referred to her job title for those who requested it. She was his right-hand person. Booking visits, arranging travel, and providing public relations for the events he would be attending.

The conversation took a more serious tone when Robin inquired, "I'm just curious why you don't require a fee to attend these events? I remember the event near Rhodes when I first met you. You didn't even pass a collection plate. It is probably none of my business to ask, but how do we pay for everything?"

Nathan laughed.

"Oh, I can see where this conversation is heading!" He said with a chuckle. "Here you are with a big fancy PHD from a big fancy college, and you feel you're worth *way* more than I pay you and want a raise, right?"

Robin gave Nathan a playful slug in the arm like two siblings fighting over the last bite of chocolate in the candy bowl.

In order to ease her concerns, Nathan explained to her, "Robin, Nathan Peerless Ministries is like we are missionaries. Missionaries get their financial support from private donations, fund raising and churches that believe in what the missionary is doing." He continued, "We have our support. Some of our private donors contribute very faithfully to our ministry. Plus, Rolling Stone is paying me very handsomely for the feature article it wants to do about my ministry. I'm not sure Rolling Stone is the absolute best vehicle to spread God's miracles or message, but I'm gonna do it anyway. Besides, this ministry is not about wealth, it's about faith and miracles."

Nathan put his arm around Robin's shoulder and placed his leg next to hers as if to make it appear he was keeping her warm. He was excited to have her with him now and looked forward to having her with him when they would eventually arrive back in Colorado. He understood she was a city girl at heart. She never wore blue jeans and country music was out of the question. He hoped, if this relationship went forward to where he wanted it to go, that this girl could be converted from floral wallpaper to *knotty pine*.

He was a simple man but with a divine gift. He needed somebody in his life to share the simple pleasures and treasures of Colorado.

Robin reached up to the hand draped across her shoulder. She grasped the fingers with hers and gazed into Nate's eyes. She leaned into his side to gather his warmth and said, "So, can I get that raise then?"

They kissed until the waiter interrupted them with the dinner check.

CHAPTER 7
ROLLING STONE

18 Months Ago

Keith Weathers feared the worst. The coughing attacks had become more frequent, and he was now seeing blood. He hated doctors almost as much as music agents. Appointments with either one made him cringe. Knowing that he would be required to be poked and prodded, not to mention the lack of privacy by some rogue medical staff, despite laws to protect this privacy, and he knew they would make the knowledge of whatever illness he had available to the media, so Keith chose a doctor in Germany to be as far away from his circle of life in Nashville, Tennessee, as possible. After several secret trips to Europe, he sat in the Munich office of Dr. Otto Schmitz waiting for the results.

Dr. Schmitz was very fluent in English so there was no language communication barrier with which Keith must contend. Unfortunately, bad news in any language is still bad news and stage four lung cancer was not the news Keith wanted to hear, but it is what he had suspected.

The diagnosis offered a very small number of treatments. Dr. Schmitz recommended an aggressive experimental treatment that had just been approved for test patients in the United States, and based on Keith's ability to pay, he could arrange for Keith to be in on those test trials.

As he boarded his private jet to travel back to Nashville, Keith was angry. He had worked hard and suffered much to achieve the fame and success he had. This just wasn't fair. He knew in his heart that his days were numbered, as this experimental treatment was yielding only about a 10% remission rate. If only there was a way to *buy* himself into a cure. There was also the chance that the clinic that was running the tests would now leak to the media that the famed Keith Weathers of Nashville Amusements, the largest promoter in the music and entertainment industries, was part of that trial. He just wasn't sure that was the type of publicity he wanted. "My God, Keith," he thought to himself, "this is your life you're talking about. Why would you worry about your vanity?"

He was extremely tired and glad he was now airborne in his private jet. He grabbed a pillow as he laid down on the sofa that only a man with considerable wealth could have on a jet. Or perhaps the President of the United States, which Keith had often wondered if he should run for office. The power would be nice, he thought. Tucking the pillow up and into his neck to keep his head slightly elevated but comfortable enough to sleep, he glanced over at a side table next to the sofa.

On the table lay the newest issue of *Rolling Stone* magazine. Keith rarely did anything but quickly shuffle through the magazine unless it was an article about him and his company, or one of his stable of stars. For some reason the cover caught his eye. The caption read:

Meet the Rock Star of Evangelists

Healing On Demand

Adorning the cover was a photo of Nathan Peerless. He was kneeling with a man in front of him. His eyes were closed, and his left arm was extended out with the index finger touching the man on his chest. Keith was intrigued by what he saw and decided to delay his nap just long enough to open the magazine and turn to the article. As he started to read the article, the first sentence began with:

Vincent Aguirre was leaving his doctor's office three months after being diagnosed with stage 4 lung cancer. This visit was different for Vincent. Most of his recent visits had been nothing but bad news about the aggressiveness of the cancer. Then, three weeks prior to this visit, he attended a Nathan Peerless Ministry event. At this event, Vincent received the touch of Nathan himself. This doctor's visit delivered some unexpected news, and that news was that Vincent was cancer free!

Keith had often had premonitions about adding different types of personalities and entertainers other than those in the music industry. "Evangelist" had entered his mind lately, but his ideas were quickly shot down by his board of directors because evangelists were never eager to lose control of their brands. He believed this type of departure from what had worked so well for him in the past might be too much of a risk and perhaps the Board were correct in their observations. But Nathan Peerless joining the stable of Nashville Amusements was now beginning to make sense to Keith. Keith read the first few sentences of the article at least twenty times. After the twenty first time, he put down the magazine and hit the buzzer connecting him to the cockpit.

"Yes, Keith, what can I do for you?" his pilot answered.

Keith replied, "Get me an outside line to David Greene."

CHAPTER 8
ASSIGNMENT

He loathed fancy restaurants with huge picture windows that allowed everybody on the outside, who couldn't afford to eat there, to look in at all the fancy white linens with the fancy crystal water glasses and all the fancy people dining in their Sunday best.

"I can afford to eat here now," David Greene thought to himself, "but you will never find me doing it." He found it ridiculous to pay fifty dollars for a bottle of wine that he could buy for just twelve. Still, this is where people dined that wanted to impress someone, although he wondered how anybody would be impressed by a twelve-dollar bottle of wine?

People made reservations to eat at Topper's Table months in advance. It was where you went to see or be seen. David could certainly see his boss's prized asset, Bobby Kamp, just fine from where he stood on the sidewalk, just outside of the outdoor dining area of the restaurant. A guest that had obviously made reservations a long time ago to impress a date, or perhaps future in-laws, got lucky tonight because dining at the restaurant was Golden Globe award winning actor, Bobby Kamp.

The stranger carefully walked over to where Bobby was seated and eating his expensive ala carte lettuce wedge with French dressing, hoping to get a coveted autograph. David watched as Bobby laid down his fancy white linen napkin on the table, smiled at the man, and politely signed his name to a piece of paper that no doubt said something to the effect;

Best wishes to my friend, Joe Smuck. Your buddy and favorite actor, Bobby "Sharky" Kamp.

Sucking down the last bit of the flavored ICEE he had bought from the 7-Eleven down the street from the restaurant, David looked for a trash can to deposit the empty cup. "Of course, a place this fancy wouldn't have trash, so why would they need a trash can," David smirked. Across from Bobby and at the same table sat one of the biggest agents in Movies and Television, Leonard Pierce. David admired Leonard because he was ruthless. Stealing other agencies' assets was common for Leonard and he was good at it. If it weren't for the fact that Leonard never signed an unknown actor in his entire career that became a star, he would have left him alone no matter what his boss needed him to do.

Leonard sat across the table from the star of the number one television show for the last four years. The show, *"Sharky"* was an old time Mafioso series with a comedic twist. David often wondered how a show about the Mafia could have comedy, but fans seemed to love it. They loved Bobby's character.

Bobby was nothing but a two-bit actor before Keith Weathers and Nashville Amusements signed him. The part was perfect for Bobby Kamp, and Keith Weathers knew it was! The rest was history. What was intended to be an eight-episode summer fill in, became a hit show, and won Bobby the *globe*. Now he sat at the table of agent Leo Pierce at the famed Topper's Table Restaurant, listening to Leo spill his guts about how signing with him as an agent would make him twice the star he was now. Leo was most likely convincing Bobby that the next step he could expect by leaving Nashville Amusements, was an Academy Award! David had seen and heard it all before.

Once the fancy dinner was over, Bobby chugged down his brandy, tossed his fancy linen napkin on the table and stood up and shook Leo Pierce's hand. Most likely telling Leo that he would mull over the offer to abandon Nashville Amusements to embark on the next step of his career.

David knew it was now time for him to go to work. The work that he was so good at. He strolled over to the nineteen-year-old kid that worked as the valet parking attendant and grabbed the kid by his arm. "See that guy getting up at that table," David said as he pointed directly at Bobby Kamp.

"Sure, He's Bobby Kamp the TV star!"

David slipped a hundred-dollar bill in the kid's hand. "Bobby Kamp is a good friend of mine. We go way back, so hand me the keys to his car and I'll go bring it to him. Boy will he ever be surprised!" The kid handed the keys to Bobby's Jaguar XJ to David, and he patted the kid on the back. David climbed in the Jaguar and started it up. He thought to himself that he deserved to drive this type of car. Perhaps he would be able to afford one someday, but for now it was a sweet experience to drive Bobby's. As usual, David's timing was impeccable as he pulled up to the valet station at Topper's Table just as Bobby arrived to take possession of his car.

David popped open the passenger side door and invited Bobby to get in. "Who in the hell are you," Bobby inquired of the man driving his car?

"Get in Bobby," David insisted! "Let's just say that Keith Weathers, our mutual employer, has requested that you and I have a little chat!"

Bobby was extremely hesitant about David's request but opted to agree to enter. The primary persuader was the Glock 9MM handgun that David was pointing directly at him.

"I have never met you before," Bobby nervously said as David peeled out from the curb and accelerated down the street.

"No, we haven't met before," David replied, "but Keith Weathers and I are very familiar with the business methods deployed by Leo Pierce who was your dinner partner tonight. I am just here to remind you that you are *obligated* to Nashville Amusements! Do we seem to have a problem with that, *Sharky?*"

With that statement David slid the barrel of the gun closer to Bobby Kamp's left temple. Obviously a very nervous and shaking Bobby Kamp paused a moment as he stared straight ahead.

"How did you know I was having dinner with Leo Pierce tonight," Bobby nervously asked?

"Let's just say that Keith Weathers makes it his business to be informed on what his clients are doing," David replied.

"No, no problem at all, sir. I am very happy with Nashville Amusements. I owe everything to them," a frightened Bobby Kamp said with a tremble in his voice.

David Greene managed to coincide Bobby Kamp's new found pleasure in Nashville Amusements with pulling the Jaguar into the circular driveway of the home belonging to Bobby. Getting out of the car David threw the keys onto Bobby's lap. "Thank you for letting me drive your car tonight, Mr. Kamp," David sarcastically said.

Bobby watched the bald, muscular man walk to the edge of his driveway and a short minute later enter a black SUV that was occupied with other characters that clearly coordinated their arrival back at his home. Bobby sighed and laid his head back to look at the ceiling of his Jaguar. He spoke to himself, "Holy Cow, this should make me get a better insight into my character!"

Bobby Kamp and Nashville Amusements would be joined at the hip for a long, long time. The next morning Bobby called Leo Pierce to thank him again for dinner, but to tell him he was going to remain loyal to Keith Weathers. Unfortunately, all Bobby Kamp could do was leave a message.

Leo Pierce had been assaulted and severely beat up by some unknown assailants after leaving Topper's Table the night before. It would be several weeks in a local hospital before Leo listened to the message.

David Greene sat at the large walnut conference table patiently waiting for his boss to come into the room. When his phone had rung in the middle of the night, with Keith calling from his private jet requesting that he must meet with him first thing in the morning, he knew it was urgent. He hated these meetings. More than likely, he had a task for him to do that wasn't going to be pleasant. These tasks never were, and he wished he had gone to college and become smart. Smart like a doctor or lawyer. If he were smart, he could be the boss, and call on others to be *his* henchman.

Sports were always more important to him than studies and that's why he excelled at them. Football was his best sport, and helped develop his body into the physical shape he was in today. A muscular specimen that intimidated everybody that he met.

His legs ached from the workout he did this morning. David sighed; took a sip of water from the bottle he was offered by the receptionist on the 7th floor. He thought to himself that this conference table appeared to be genuine walnut. He didn't know much about the different species of wood, having never ventured into carpentry, but this grain was beautiful. David could tell the difference between laminate and real. The leather chairs that went with this table were pure Italian leather. His employer obviously had money. They probably didn't use this conference room often, but obviously spared no expense on the furnishings to impress whoever might be invited in.

Upon hearing the elevator bell produce the ding that announced its arrival on the 7th floor, David knew it was his boss finally arriving for the requested meeting. He stood and turned to face the door of the conference room. A slender man of approximately five foot ten inches with some slight gray around his temples and a mustache to match, entered the room where David stood. He was accompanied by a man with a larger build, and less hair. Both men, he guessed, were in their late fifties. They smiled at David and proceeded with the pleasantries of the greeting.

"Nice to finally meet you David," said the dark-haired man. "Is it okay to call you David?" He added.

David assured the man that being on a first name basis was certainly fine with him. Friendly gestures like this meant that he was in far better standing with these two men than most of the characters they commanded.

"Please call me Keith. Mr. Weathers is what everybody called my father," He replied not meaning to be contrite.

"Very good, Keith," David accepted.

Extending his hand to shake David's, the overweight man in the dark suit said, "Hi David, my name is Ron. Ron LeGrand."

All three men sat down at the table with David across from the other two. He wasn't sure it was just his imagination, but Keith and Ron seemed to be elevated above him.

Keith Weathers was the President and CEO of Nashville Amusements, LLC. Once an aspiring singer, songwriter, in his youth, Keith discovered just how tough it was to make it in the music business. It was a dirty business with sinister men that controlled it. What he found out from the struggle to survive in the music business was he had a knack for finding talent and promoting and growing that talent into a money-making star. That is how his company grew into the multi-billion-dollar company it became.

Ron LeGrand was the money guy for Nashville Amusements. He kept his finger on the pulse of the money and answered only to Keith. David Greene's place in all of this was head of security. Not only for NA, but also for many of Keith's rising stars. He did everything from setting up security at events and concerts, being a personal bodyguard to many of Keith's *assets*, as he called them, and helping *sway* those assets back to camp *if* they might want to wander away from Nashville Amusements. David had gained the reputation for being the best *persuader* in the biz and had never let one of Keith's assets venture away.

"David, you're looking very fit," Keith offered. "I like it when my employees stay in shape, don't get soft!" David sensed that Ron LeGrand might not be enjoying this conversation.

Keith went on to explain that the reason they had called David to meet with them today was they needed his expertise in *persuasion*! There was a difference in this assignment. This time, the job wasn't an *asset*, yet!

CHAPTER 9
PROPOSAL

The sun was setting on a Colorado sky that was so beautiful that Nate felt God was out there on the horizon painting it himself. He didn't want the day to end. The dishes were clinking in the kitchen sink, and he wondered just how much Robin hated him right now for living in a house without a dishwasher. He chuckled as he considered that Robin might not have done the dishes, anywhere, at any time, in her life.

She appeared on the cabin porch a few minutes later to join Nate. He watched her walk out to where he was sitting and admired just how beautiful she was. Sitting down beside him Nathan thanked her for doing the dishes in this harsh country environment.

"How do you live like this?" Robin questioned as she laughed.

Nathan was glad that their recent revival tour was done. He loved seeing different parts of the country and meeting those people that love Jesus, but even God needed to rest. He certainly needed to rest, and having Robin join him for that rest, in Colorado, was even better! Looking into her eyes, he adored their beauty despite the layer of mascara. Her designer jeans with heels were not what he would consider comfortable or country! Still, none of this mattered to him because they were together, and he was falling in love with her.

"Robin," he asked, "do you, ever see yourself loving these mountains as much as I do?"

She replied "Well, no!"

Once the feeling of being shell shocked by her answer settled in a bit, he retorted, "Okay, I guess that ends this conversation." Sadness was etched upon his face when Robin reached her tender hand to Nathan's face and spoke softly, "My dear Nathan, what I meant to say was *nobody* could love these mountains as much as you do. But *because* you do, and *because* I care for you, I could love anywhere that you are."

He felt exonerated by her statement. Upon hearing Robin's confession that his comfort and peace were enough for her, Nathan's next step was clear. Nathan's voice trembled slightly as he placed his faded blue jean knee on the rustic wood floor of his mountain cabin porch and asked, "Then, do you also think you could live with the last name of Peerless?"

It was her turn to be shell shocked. This was not expected. She felt tears well up in her eyes and she gazed down at Nathan staring up at her holding a diamond ring and asked, "Is this a proposal?"

"Sure is," Nathan replied.

He rose and they came together and hugged. The kiss was so epic that had a bystander walked by and witnessed the event, they might have blushed. Once the euphoria of the proposal had subsided, Nathan and Robin began discussing their future together, they agreed the engagement needn't be long, but there were many people and things to consider before a wedding date could be set. Agreeing to just enjoy the night and sleep on it before getting into details, they sat and held each other. As was her usual fashion, Robin turned the splendor of the evening back to Nathan Peerless Ministry.

"Nate," she spoke, "I know you wanted to show me around Colorado tomorrow, but I need to go into Denver."

"Denver?" he inquired.

Robin explained "It's my job to keep NPM moving along and I received a phone call from a potential contributor. A *financial* contributor!" She continued, "We need to get our support up so we can afford this luxurious cabin."

Nathan smiled despite understanding the sarcasm of her statement. He inquired "Who are you meeting and where?"

Robin answered "His name is Keith Weathers with Nashville something or other. He said he's a fan of NPM and has an idea to help us. We're meeting at his Denver bank on Sixteenth Street," Robin added.

"Well, please remember the ministry isn't about money," Nathan offered.

"But you must admit, asking to meet at *his* bank is very appealing," Robin replied.

Robin inquired as to what Nathan's plans were for tomorrow since she would be gone most of the day. Nathan yawned, stood up and stretched, preparing to walk to his bedroom to engage in much needed sleep and responded, "I'm going to see some friends of mine here in Evergreen. Their dog just had puppies and I'm going to go look at them."

"A *puppy*" she thought. Just what they needed, a puppy!

"I hope and pray it's a female," Robin thought to herself.

CHAPTER 10
THE GIFT

28 years ago

Climbing up the stairs of the yellow school bus that he was late for every morning, Nate's best friend and confidant, Robert Tyree, motioned for him to come sit next to him. With a half scowl and half smile, the bus driver, Paul Merrifield, blurted out for Nate to hurry up and sit down so he could get going or they would all be late for school.

Nate loved Paul. He knew deep down that he could never be angry with him. Paul was his Sunday School teacher and, despite not having any children of his own, Nate had an affection for Paul much like a grandchild for his grandpa.

"Saved you a seat, Nate. Ned wanted to sit by me, but I told him you had to. Told him that you were helping me pass the quiz in math class today," Robert explained the fib that left the seat open for Nate to assume.

Nate looked at his friend with an air of being flabbergasted. "Geesh, Bobby, Ned had to know you were lying. Nobody on God's green earth could help you pass math class!" The boys chuckled at Nate's exposé, and he settled in on their bench seat as the bus pulled out into the roadway that would lead to Jackson Middle School.

A school that, by any standard, would be considered small. With only 104 students, every kid knew every other, and, as a matter of fact, every family knew every other, and every mom and dad in this mountain town wanted their child to be friends with Nathan Peerless. At thirteen years old, he was different. Not strange, just a wholesome, polite kid that actively exposed his love for the Lord.

"You got any news on whether Amy Richardson is gonna go to the fall dance with you?" Robert prodded for the inside scoop from his friend.

Nate smiled what might be construed as a sinister smile. "Of course she said yes. I'm Nate Peerless, you fool." With an excited and jerky movement, Robert playfully punched at Nate in revelation of the news.

The mood turned serious between the boys when they noticed Amy staring back at their antics with a look of scorn. Nate realized he had probably violated some unwritten rule and probably should have left their upcoming date a secret.

Turning his gaze from the scorn of Amy Richardson, Nate looked out the bus window at the fall colors beginning their emergence onto the aspen tree leaves of Evergreen. He wasn't quite sure why he loved this time of year. Perhaps it was the beautiful colors that the dying leaves produced. Maybe it was the smell of smoke in the evening air as families gathered around a fire. That smell that the firewood, as it consumed its fuel and wafted about a person's nostrils, created to provide a uniqueness compared to any other aroma.

Regardless of the nice distraction, he knew he would have to seek out forgiveness from Amy just as soon as they got off the bus. She was the most beautiful girl he had ever known. Getting her to accept his invitation to the fall dance was a triumph that any pubescent boy would relish for the rest of their lives.

Nate's attention returned to reality, feeling the bus swerving ever so slightly. He saw nothing on the road that would require it to be maneuvered in this manner. He looked up at Paul to try and get a glimpse of what he was doing. Just as he focused in on the mirror that allowed Paul to glance back at his passengers, Nate noticed that Paul was grasping at his chest while attempting to control the steering wheel.

The next thing Nate knew he had been hurtled to the other side of the bus which was now lying completely on that side. His head hurt as he reached up to examine if any blood had been produced from where he felt the pain. His hand didn't produce any sign of blood, but he could hear the screams and cries of his fellow classmates, two of whom he was now intertwined with, having landed on them when the bus went over.

There were books and papers strewn all about the bus. His arm hurt and, with all the strength he could manage, he grabbed the back of the bench seat that had been in front of him, and he was able to free himself from the other boys. He hoisted himself up to perch on the edge of the bench seat that was now horizontal to the front of the bus.

Nate had been sitting closer to the front of the bus and, helping other crying classmates up, he traversed the distance to the front to find Paul strapped into his seatbelt with his head down and showing no signs of being coherent. Nate thought to himself, "Just how are we going to get out of here?" The door to the entrance of the bus was on the side that was now against the ground and couldn't be opened. He knew Paul was in desperate need of help.

Luck had it that a local resident had seen the bus go into the road embankment and flip on its side. He ran up to the driver's side windshield and pounded it. "I'm going to get help, kids. You'll be alright. I'll be back with help as quick as I can!" Nate was glad he had come to help, but he was scared that he was leaving them.

His arm hurt almost as badly as his head. Nate rubbed it and wondered if it might be broken. He knew he couldn't worry about himself. Paul was unconscious and a slight blue tint had appeared on his skin. With his good arm and hand, Nate gently shook him hoping for some kind of response indicating that he would be okay. Unable to get a response from Paul, Nate's focus turned to his classmates.

"Help is coming, guys! Hang in there! It'll be okay." He wasn't sure if his calling out helped because he couldn't be heard at the back of the bus with all the crying. Then Nate heard the sound he longed to hear, sirens.

In what seemed like an eternity before first responders could get the rear of the bus opened and begin assisting kids out that portal, Nate began to pray. He prayed hard for God to protect his classmates and for nobody to be seriously injured. The bulk of his prayer was for his friend, Sunday school teacher, and school bus driver, Paul.

When the fireman finally reached Nate, who had his good arm draped around Paul's neck so it acted like a pillow, he asked the fireman to help Paul first. "Please, get him out! He's not doing so good. I can get out and I'll follow you."

Paul wasn't a small man, and it took three firemen to grab him by his arms and feet to maneuver the distance to the back of the bus. Once they had Paul freed from the wreckage, Nate exited right behind him. One of the firemen threw a blanket around Nate's shoulders, although he didn't understand why. He wasn't cold.

"C'mon, son, you're very brave to stay with your friend. It looks like you're hurt. Let's get you to the ambulance." The fireman insisted that Nate follow him. Nate turned to follow him to the ambulance when out of the corner of his eye he could see several of the firemen taking turns pressing on Paul's chest. They would cup their lips to Paul's, breathe puffs of air into his mouth, then begin pressing on his chest.

Nate watched as one of the firemen that had been pressing on Paul's chest stood up and proclaimed to the other firemen around him, "It's no good, guys. No pulse. He's gone." A tear came to Nate's eye and began to drip down his cheek. He understood what the fireman had just professed. His friend was dead. "Let's go, son, we need to tend to your injuries," the fireman that had been escorting Nate encouraged him in a polite manner.

He felt terrible. He loved Paul Merrifield. More than his stepfather. Paul had been more of a positive influence than his stepfather could ever hope to be. Nate didn't hate him; he just didn't have the love of the Lord that Paul had. An ambulance driver instructed Nate to sit on the gurney so they could load him into the ambulance, just as the parents of his fellow classmates, upon hearing news of the accident, began to arrive in panic about their children.

Then, Nate heard it.

A voice in his head as clear as day.

"Go to him, Nate. He is only sleeping. You have prayed and I have listened. Go now and lay your hands upon his chest."

He knew immediately he must obey the command. Nate knew from where the commandment had come. He jumped from the ambulance gurney, evoking the displeasure of the attendant, and streaked to where Paul was laying on the ground.

He knelt on both knees.

Despite his one arm piercing with pain, Nate placed his hands upon Paul's chest. The parents that had come to claim their children at this tragic scene watched in awe. Swirling about Nate were sparkles of color. Greens, reds, oranges, and yellows. Just like the fall leaves. They swirled until Nate and Paul were no longer visible amongst them.

Then a flash of light, so bright it appeared like a firework on the Fourth of July. The firemen, ambulance workers, parents and Nate's classmates watched as all color and brightness faded.

All that was left of the spectacle was Nate, who had removed his hands from Paul's chest, and Paul, with natural color having returned to his face and normal breaths of air filling his lungs. A fireman bent down to check the pulse of Paul Merrifield and called out to an ambulance worker, "Get me the gurney and some oxygen. We need to get this man to the hospital, pronto! This man is alive!"

Nate stood and looked out at the crowd that had just witnessed the event. He wasn't sure that they knew that it wasn't just an event they had just observed; it was a miracle.

The two faces he was the happiest to see were his best friend, Robert, and the smiling face of Amy, his date to the fall dance.

The doctor came into the examination room at Evergreen Hospital. Pulling back the curtain that had served as Nate's only privacy, the doctor peered out from over his reading glasses. "You're a lucky boy, my lad. The ambulance people thought you might have a concussion and a broken arm.

Well, all the x-rays are negative. You're fine," the doctor proclaimed as if he was the reason for the health of Nate.

He noticed his head no longer hurt, nor did his arm. "Guess God took care of me when he healed Paul. Makes sense, he is an awesome God," Nate thought as he smiled.

"Your parents are here. You're free to go home," the doctor said.

Nate hopped off the hospital examination table, but before the doctor had turned to leave, Nathan made a request. "Can I see Paul before I leave?"

The doctor stared at him over the half-moon reading glasses and responded, "I guess it'll be okay. The man's remarkable. He's awake and alert and shows no residual effects from what we thought was a heart attack. Very remarkable."

Nate was escorted down a hallway by one of the nurses and entered the room where his friend, Paul, was lying on a bed with several wires hooked to monitors. The glow on Paul's face brought delight to Nate.

"Come here, my dear boy. I understand it will be difficult with all these wires attached to me, but I need to give you a hug."

Nate walked over to Paul and bent over to apply a much-desired embrace. Nate felt tears swelling in his eyes but held back an open sob of joy. Afterall, he was thirteen years old and thirteen-year-old boys didn't cry.

Paul reached up to touch the face of Nate as he spoke. "I'm so sorry, Nathan. I could have seriously hurt you and all the children."

"Nobody was seriously hurt. Well, maybe except you," Nate answered in earnest. Paul smiled a broad smile back at Nate.

With a slight tremor in his voice, Paul spoke, "You know, Nathan, I understand what happened. God healed me through you. I had left my body and was hovering above it when you came to me and knelt. When you touched my chest, I could see your hands deep inside me. Your hands touched my heart, and God made it start beating again. He used you, my boy. He used you to save my life and give me a second chance."

Nate beamed a smile. "Ya know, Paul, he must have had a reason. I'm not sure why he used me, but I can't wait to see what he has in store for you," Nate spoke with compassion and love that his friend relished.

"Nate, I don't know if you know what I'm going to tell you, and I may not look the part, but I'm a very wealthy man. God told you to go to me and he used you to heal me. Now, what I believe God has told me is, I'm meant to assist you in your mission for him, our Lord and Savior, Jesus Christ."

Nate seemed astonished and puzzled by what Paul had just told him, "And just *what* is that mission, Paul?"

"That God is in control. He is love. He can use people in remarkable ways. He wants you to bring people to salvation through blood atonement and resurrection. He wants you to use your gift."

Even more puzzled, Nate pressed him for an answer, "What gift?"

"The touch of Nathan Peerless, my boy, the touch of Nathan Peerless," Paul spoke with all the wisdom of the ages.

Fall came and went and with every change of the seasons, Nathan grew into a man. A man that, based on the testimony of the witnesses of the miracle at the bus crash, became ever increasing in demand for his time. First, his reputation grew among the local mountain churches around Evergreen, Colorado, and then into the Colorado plains of Denver and into the Midwest.

Paul understood that Nathan's *gift* wouldn't stop being in demand around their region. He knew that soon Nathan would be in demand on a national scale. He also understood that healing wasn't Nathan's only gift. Nathan was endowed by the Lord to preach. When God hadn't spoken to Nathan to heal an illness or affliction at a church meeting or revival, he provided Nathan with the gift to spread the word of the gospel.

Nathan had the ability to touch souls, not only with his hands but with his words.

Money never forbade Nathan from doing the work of the Lord. Paul made sure of that, and he financed every trip. This made Nathan even more in demand. When Nathan had time to rest, which was infrequent, he would always return to the mountain retreat of Paul's mountain cabin.

After a long tour of the Pacific Northwest, Nathan returned home to find his friend in ill health. As they sat on the front porch reminiscing about the triumphs of Nathan's recent trip, Paul turned the conversation to a serious tone. "Nathan, during my recent visit with my cardiologist, we discussed the results of the tests he had me do. The prognosis wasn't good. I don't mean to worry you. That's not my motive for discussing my health with you. It's just, I believe you ought to know that my time in this body is coming to an end."

Nathan shifted his chair to be close to where Paul was sitting. With an intensive stare, Nathan reached over and took Paul's hand in his.

"Not this time, my friend. God has not anointed you to heal me. There will be no miracle performed this time. God expects me to come home soon and I'm ready," Paul explained with an earnest and joyful expression in his voice and on his face.

Knowing that Paul was telling the truth, Nathan could only continue to hold Paul's hand and rejoice in the friendship God had brought to each of them.

A week later, Nathan said the eulogy at Paul's funeral at Evergreen Evangelical Church. It was attended by over three hundred people and Nathan recognized many who had been at the miracle at the bus crash.

He walked up the steps to the porch of the cabin on County Road 29 and turned to look down the gravel road that led up to it. What had been Paul's cabin was now Nathan's. Paul had left everything in his will to Nathan, including the cabin. The fortune he received in Paul's will, and was now the steward for, would provide for Nathan Peerless Ministry for many generations to come. The money was nice, and Nathan was extremely grateful for the gift he had been left, but the simple cabin was the true gift and would always be his bastion of peace when troubled times came.

CHAPTER 11
DARKNESS DESCENDING

She encouraged Nathan to retire for the evening, as several times during their conversation his eyes had begun to droop. He agreed with her that he could no longer fight his fatigue and decided that going to his room to sleep was the best option. He loved spending any time with her, but the recent tour had been a long and arduous venture, and he needed to sleep.

Robin could hear Nathan snoring just as soon as he laid down on his bed. She chuckled that it seemed like he might have started sleeping before he ever hit the bed. As tired as she was too, she opted to sit out on the porch of the cabin and let her mind relax before she retired for the night.

Pulling a warm woolen blanket around her, she thought this would be a blanket she wouldn't ever purchase. It was red and green plaid, and it had seen better days. This was the type of blanket a bachelor would own. A man with simple tastes, unlike her.

Her upbringing had never been simple. She came from a family where her parents lived beyond their means. They would never show it, and it was important to her mother that Robin always appeared to be from a well-to-do family. Her mother was a beauty queen and regularly won several of the state pageants. She required Robin to succeed her in the pageant arena once her time as a contestant was over.

Unlike her mother, besides her beauty, Robin had no recognizable talent. Her extreme beauty just wasn't enough to woo the judges into making her a finalist. Her father was an accountant. He had a good job and was well liked by people. The only problem with his profession was wealth didn't follow it.

The arguments about the cost to keep Robin in the pageants became commonplace in her family environment. So much so that her parents split and ended their marriage. When she reached the time to decide if she would attend college or make her way in the working world, Robin decided on college, having received a full ride scholarship from Rhodes College.

Realizing that the brisk fall mountain air of Evergreen was getting too chilly for her, she threw off the blanket and placed it neatly on the chair on which she had been sitting. Walking into the cabin, the fireplace still had the glow of the embers that remained from an earlier fire. She placed a couple of logs on the embers and they quicky ignited. Grabbing another blanket off the back of the couch, she covered herself and laid her head on a couch pillow.

The last thing she thought of before succumbing to the rigors of the day was that her relationship with Nathan would never be like her parents had. There would always be enough money. She might not have had any talents to win pageants, but she would make sure she used her beauty to ensure they always had enough money.

Robin arrived at the First National Bank of Colorado at precisely 10:00 in the morning. She valued promptness and loathed anybody that didn't. Checking in at the receptionist's desk, she was pleased to learn that her meeting party was already in the bank conference room waiting for her. "This is a good start," Robin thought as she pulled out a compact from her purse to take one last look that her makeup was in order. As she entered the meeting room, three men rose to their feet to greet her, and she politely extended her hand to shake each of theirs. Keith Weathers took the lead, providing the introductions.

"Ms. Gunderson, it's such a pleasure to meet you. I'm Keith Weathers of Nashville Amusements. I'm the one who spoke to you on the phone," he beamed a welcoming smile as he extended a cordial greeting.

"My pleasure, Mr. Weathers" Robin responded politely.

"Oh, please, call me by my first name. Mr. Weathers was my father," Keith said in his usual manner. "These are my associates, Ron LeGrand and David Greene."

She wasn't sure what she expected when she accepted Keith's invitation to meet him. He wasn't as tall as she had envisioned and was much more slender than she had imagined. With a bushy mustache that seemed to overtake his upper lip and eyes that looked a little too close to each other. He didn't wear a suit but had nicely pressed blue jeans, adorned by alligator cowboy boots. Not what she had expected.

Robin smiled and replied, "Good morning, gentlemen, pleasure to meet all of you."

David Greene was blown away with just how attractive Robin Gundersen was and couldn't remember any assignment that was this easy on the eyes. Keith Weathers did not appear to show any of the teenage-boy-gawking that David did and took the lead to conduct this meeting in a professional way. He got right to the point with Robin.

"Robin, Nashville Amusements represents a great number of talented groups and individuals in the music, television, and film industries. We maintain a documented retention rate of 98% of our clients. This is an unprecedented rate. How do we do this?" he asked.

Robin felt his opening introduction appeared to be slightly scripted and rehearsed.

Keith continued with his presentation, "We do this by being fair with our clients! They feel they have a voice in their direction. And they do!"

Robin listened as Keith explained that Nashville Amusements wanted to help promote Nathan Peerless Ministry, to provide the resources to reach as many people as humanly possible. "No," he said, "as many people as is *godly* possible. Why would we want to do this?" Keith posed the question, paused for a moment of silence, then proceeded to answer his own question. "Because we have seen the incredible Nathan Peerless heal people, and we believe the *world* needs this man!"

He continued to explain that with Nashville supporting and handling the ministry, that their troubles were over. No longer would Nathan or Robin need to worry about money, travel, events and most importantly, security. Keith pointed to David Greene and explained, "Nathan Peerless will definitely need security. It's inevitable that some *crazy* will attack Nathan someday! David Greene here will make sure that doesn't happen!"

Robin eyed Keith Weathers with skepticism. She wondered why a company that handled and promoted musicians and actors would want to do the same for an evangelist/faith healer. Still, her mind couldn't help retreating to the money problems that defeated her parents.

Robin replied to the men seated before her with an earnest question, "I'm not really sure what's in this for you? Nate's a different breed from what you're used to, and I do a decent job at keeping Nate busy." Robin couldn't attest that she did a decent job controlling the money though, because she didn't. Nate did that, and always provided the funds when she needed to pay for things.

Keith motioned to Ron LeGrand, who, with the dip of his hand, reached in and pulled an envelope from his suit jacket and handed it to Robin. Looking at the envelope, she could tell it held a check. She opened the envelope and glanced at a check made out to Nathan Peerless Ministry. At first, she thought it was a mistake, but her eyes focused on the amount of the check, and she brought her eyes up to look directly into Keith Weathers.

"I make it my business to understand the needs of my clients. This is why they come to us to help them." He continued to explain that the check she held in her hand was only a *signing* bonus. "There is far more than that in Nathan's future. And yours," Keith moved toward closing the deal.

It was more money than she could've imagined.

He offered to let her think about what they had talked about. To go back up the mountain to discuss it with Nathan. Perhaps he would want to meet with Keith himself. Regardless, she could have some time to consider the future, together with Nashville Amusements.

As Robin prepared to depart out the door of the meeting room, Keith chimed in with the last part of his pitch. He spoke directly to her as he shook her hand in farewell and said, "It's also my business to know my clients in a very personal way, Robin. I know weddings can be very expensive!"

Robin was stunned as she left the meeting. How in the world could he know about her and Nate's engagement? This made her feel uncomfortable, but it soon passed as she pondered everything the ministry could do with the check she had received from Nashville Amusements and Keith Weathers.

She also pondered how she would approach Nate with what she considered to be the opportunity of a lifetime.

CHAPTER 12
CHOICES

Standing in a metal pen with a straw floor, Nathan was surrounded. The attack was relentless. Defenseless, he couldn't imagine how anything could be as cute as these seven pups all seeking his attention. He was also convinced he couldn't pick just one of these little animals, so he might have to take all seven! Chuckling to himself, he decided this might be too much for Robin to accept, after all, he was in the infancy of turning her from an urban princess into a mountain girl.

Maybe he should reconsider getting a puppy at all. He really hadn't discussed it with Robin and perhaps he had alienated her by even suggesting he was going to look at his neighbor's dogs.

Nathan, who had squatted down to become less imposing to the young puppies, stood erect and turned to his neighbors, Jim and Martha Cook. He laughed as he spoke, "Golly, Jim, I appreciate it that you would consider asking me to take one of these adorable creatures."

Jim responded, "Martha and I just want a good home for them. We can't imagine anybody better than you to become the *dad* to one of Sadie's babies."

"Well, my concerns are my travels with the ministry and, also, I'm not alone in this matter any longer," Nate revealed to Jim and Martha. "I'm going to be a married man soon, so that would mean this pup would have a daddy and a *mommy!*" Jim and Martha giggled at this statement and Nate tried to smile despite feeling uneasy as to the reality of what he had just said. Martha presented a revelation to Nathan, "We rarely pick our pets, often, our pets pick us!"

Nate pondered her revelation and replied, "Well, I guess if I'm going to let one of Sadie's pups pick me as their daddy, I had better home in on which of these puppies are females." He calculated that Robin would be far more accepting of this idea when she came home from Denver if he presented her with a girl dog.

Just as he convinced himself that this adoption was going to happen, he saw Martha's finger point to his feet. Looking down onto his well, worn boots, Nathan gazed upon two black eyes staring back up at him. There sat one of Sadie's pups that was jet black from head to tail. The dog's body was postured half on and half off Nate's boot with a black tail thumping on the straw floor.

Apparently, Martha Cook was right with her knowledge of the pet kingdom. This cute little puppy sitting on Nathan's boot had staked his claim on the one who would become the master. Bending over to pick up and gently cradle the puppy in his hands, Nathan lifted the animal up above his head to gather the gender information required to complete this bonding transaction.

It was too late to turn back now. This would be Nate's dog.

Robin would be getting a *boy!*

CHAPTER 13
RIGHT PLACE AT THE RIGHT TIME

Once Robin had left Keith Weathers and the others, he turned to face his accomplices in the meeting room with a smug look on his face. "Nicely done" Keith said as he nodded to David Greene. "The technology available to listen in on people is phenomenal," he added.

With the help of *spy* devices planted at the Peerless cabin in Evergreen, Keith knew he had picked the right man for the job in David Greene. David responded in kind with a nod of acceptance at Keith's praise.

These men knew that Robin was vulnerable to the lure of money. The small sampling provided in the form of a down payment seemed to overwhelm her. Keith relished this type of client. A client that could be bought.

The story of Nashville Amusements and its rise to be the leader in talent representation was all about Keith Weathers being a talented songwriter. His singing voice was adequate. In fact, it was quite good. Although he could sing and play the guitar, it was his looks that held him back. Studios didn't seem to think he had that *star* look. Still, they all liked his songs. He had a knack for rhythm and melodies that they knew would sell. In the beginning of his career, he didn't want to believe it when studio heads would tell him about the inadequacies of his appearance. He bounced from one agent to another. Most of them patronized him to get at his songs. He would get a small fee to sell his song and lyrics, and his agent would reap the financial benefit of signing a new up and coming performer with great talent and a brand-new song that had been written and sold by Keith Weathers.

The rejection was overwhelming. After years of toiling to get recognition for his music as a recording artist, Keith finally came to the realization that the music business was a fraud!

Hungry and depressed, Keith decided he would not send any more of *his* music to any agent. He just could not stand to be used. He worked odd jobs to feed himself, one of which was a sound man at a local bar in Nashville. This was the type of bar that offered new artists a chance to perform either their songs, or existing hits of famous performers. He was not working there to continue trying to crack into the business. He was working there to eat.

Keith still wrote music. He just would not share it with anybody. He often thought his music now was better than ever, but he could not stand hearing another one of his songs on the radio making somebody else rich.

One Friday evening, Keith was testing the equipment. Fridays were always a busy night at the bar, and he knew he would be busy all night long. It was not unusual for the bar to book five or six performers per night. Each artist hoping that an agent would be in the audience. Or even better, a studio executive would come backstage to sign them and propel them off to fame and fortune. A reason Keith liked working there is it made him feel good to watch these kids, full of hope, filled with desire, getting the blood sucked right out of them.

He was disgusted with himself for feeling this way, but he could not help himself. This Friday night was different. It changed the direction of life for the cynical Keith Weathers. After three performers gave it their best up on the stage, he set up for number four. A young kid of eighteen. He cradled a vintage Les Paul guitar with a hand carved shoulder strap straight out of Tandy's Leather catalog. Keith smiled. He knew this kid would crash and burn hard. He thought just how much this kid reminded him of himself when he was naïve to this dirty, dirty business.

Joe, the bar owner and announcer, asked if the kid was ready to sing and he nodded his head and said, "Yes, sir." Keith laughed to himself at just how polite this kid was. "It won't last for long," Keith mused.

Then the kid began to sing. It was not an original song, but it was an original voice. For the first time, Keith Weathers understood why he never made it in the music industry as a performer. This kid was everything Keith was not and would never be. He was Johnny Cash, Willie Nelson, Waylon Jennings, and Conway Twitty all bundled into one. A throw back to a long-gone era, but he made it sound new! Brand new. And he was good looking and fresh.

The kid finished his set of four songs and the crowd cheered for twenty minutes. Keith had never seen that happen at this bar.

Joe invited the kid back to perform at the bar the following Friday night and he graciously accepted. Keith sensed this kid was something special and decided to introduce himself.

"Hi, kid. Great job out there tonight," Keith acknowledged. "My name is Keith Weathers," he said, extending his hand out to shake the kid's hand.

The kid responded, "Nice to meet you, Mr. Weathers. My name is Cole, Cole Stanton."

"Aw, call me Keith, kid. Mr. Weathers was my father."

The friendship between Keith and Cole grew from that day forward. Keith witnessed several agents and studio execs speak to Cole, but they all stopped short of signing him until he had some original material, or they could get some for him. Keith saw that this was *his* opportunity to turn raw ore into gold, and he pounced on it. He explained to Cole that the reason he ran sound at the bar was so he could help young talent avoid the pitfalls of the business that he had experienced.

"Look, Cole, I'm not a big-time recording executive. I'm not even an agent. All I know for sure is talent when I see and hear it. I've heard those greedy suits that talk to you. They all want to sign you, but..." Keith bowed his head for a moment in heavy contemplation before continuing to speak to Cole, "What they all say is they need to get you some original music."

Cole believed Keith. Keith also had something to offer that nobody else could. He had music, and songs.

An acoustical guitar sat in a stand nearby, just in case one of the performers needed an emergency guitar, and Keith picked it up. Arranging his fingers on the frets, he began to strum and pick a melody on the guitar. Then he sang one of his songs. After he finished, Cole sat stupefied at what he had just heard.

"That was special, Keith. What d'ya call it?" Cole asked in true admiration.

Keith liked this kid. He was innocent and pure. Everything this business was not. He answered, "It's called 'Come Pull Up a Rock and Fish Awhile'. I wrote it about going fishing with my father at the lake."

"That's a special memory for you, isn't it?"

Keith smiled a strained smile. "Never went fishing with my father. He was a drunk. He was too busy drinking with his buddies to ever take me fishing."

Both Keith and Cole reflected on what had just been shared.

"Well, they say the best songs are made from the pain we all feel," Cole broke the silence.

Cole Stanton became the first client for Nashville Amusements, LLC. Cole thanked Keith Weathers at the Grammy awards for making his *Song of the Year* award possible. Three years later, Nashville Amusements moved into their new corporate headquarters as one of the largest talent representatives in the music, acting and event industries.

Keith had the Midas touch. He knew when it was right to get his hands on a talent. He could tell when a voice, face or event could make him money.

Religious events and evangelists were uncharted territory. Nobody was really talking about the *money* to be made from handling these types of talents. Keith Weathers had learned a long time ago that, if you are in the right place at the right time, everything falls in line from there. He did not believe in God, but there were lots of people that did. Lots of those people were sick, just like him, and doctors would not or could not help them. These people needed something. When he started to look at religion and the events that were being held in this country, he decided he needed to be a part of this. To have a piece.

These people that were sick or crippled needed something. They needed Nathan Peerless. They needed his touch, and they had money to spend!

Keith needed Nathan's touch, and money was no object.

CHAPTER 14
THE DARK

Driving home from his neighbor's ranch, Nathan looked at the old laundry basket that now served as a makeshift carrier for one very dark, male puppy. For the first time in a long time, he wasn't sure that he hadn't made a big mistake. The old bath towel that served to provide comfort for his newfound friend seemed enough for the dog, as he settled down for a nap on the journey to his new home. Nathan looked down at the sleeping pup and spoke softly, "Well, boy, I sure hope you get some sleep because when Robin sees you, we both might be sleeping outside in the cold and dark!"

Nathan turned up the long gravel driveway that led to his mountain cabin. He enjoyed driving his old 1996 Ford truck with vinyl seats and a rusted-out truck bed. This truck was simple, just like him. The truck would never conjure the thought of luxury with anybody, but somehow it just fit him. Just like his new dog. He had let Robin drive the newer, more luxurious SUV into Denver for her meeting with what she called Nashville *Something or other*!

He wasn't very much concerned with the results of her meeting. She felt it was about funding, but money was the least of Nathan's concerns. Seeing the SUV parked in front of the cabin meant that the inevitable was now at hand. Robin was about to meet the dog!

As Nathan stepped out of the driver's side of the truck, an eager and boisterous Robin Gundersen came springing from the cabin screen door, out onto the porch, and bounced down the steps into Nathan's arms. Nathan, startled and holding onto her tightly as to not drop her, laughed and shouted, "Well golly, sweetheart, I missed you too!"

Robin gave him a passionate kiss and responded in a joking manner, "Oh, I didn't miss you, I'm just glad the truck is okay!" He dropped her in a tease and acted indifferent to her advances. They both hugged each other in a way only people in love could do. Once all the horseplay had subsided, Nate remembered the precious cargo he had left in the laundry basket on the front seat. He motioned to Robin to make sure she closed her eyes and once he was convinced that she was complying, he moved to the other side of the truck and extracted the black puppy. Nate came around to where Robin was standing with her eyes closed and informed her that she could open her eyes now.

Those big, beautiful brown eyes opened to look upon two black eyes and a little pink tongue. She was a bit taken back with the shock of this little creature staring back at her and seemed speechless for a moment. Nathan sensed she might not be too happy with him for proceeding with selecting a pet without her.

Nathan spoke cautiously, "Ms. Gundersen, meet dog. Dog, meet your mommy."

This did the trick, and Robin couldn't help but laugh at Nate's introduction. She was reluctant to scoop up the dog in her arms and Nathan didn't push her to hold him. Nathan carried the dog up onto the porch and he and Robin sat in their selected and designated chairs as the dog played at their feet. Disappointed that Nate had chosen a male, Robin soon began to warm up to the dog to the point that she picked it up and placed it on her lap. Now that Nate sensed the crisis of the newest addition to Nathan Peerless Ministry was accepted, he decided it was a good time to inquire about the events of Robin's meeting in Denver.

They sat on the cabin porch and Robin retold the events of her day and the meeting with Keith Weathers, Ron LeGrand and David Greene. Nate was amused but skeptical as to why Nashville Amusements would be interested in moving into faith ministries. Nathan questioned Robin on what she sensed was their motivation. She answered Nathan with, "Because they love God."

"They can love God without supporting our ministry," Nathan responded.

Robin revealed the check that Ron LeGrand had handed her. "But doesn't this mean they love God a lot", Robin quizzed.

Nathan was flabbergasted by the dollar amount of the check. Robin explained, "This check is just a signing bonus. There's a lot more where this came from!"

Nathan was amused by the dollar amount of the check, but also understood that this kind of money would also carry big demands. The kind of demands that he wouldn't be able to provide. This was, after all, God's ministry, and he simply went about God's work. Not the work of men.

So as not to diminish Robin's efforts and excitement, Nate folded the check and placed it into Robin's hand. He held her hand in his as he felt the paper between their palms. Looking into Robin's eyes he spoke to her intently but with patience and emphasis. "Let me sleep on this. I need to pray and seek God's wisdom and guidance."

Robin shook her head in agreement but failed to confess to Nathan that, as his hand touched hers, with the check from Nashville Amusements placed between them, she felt odd. A feeling not unlike the day Nathan touched her temple. Except this time, she didn't feel warmth and love. This touch felt empty, cold with despair. The touch felt like darkness. Void of any light.

She was very uneasy about the sensation she had just felt and told Nate she was very tired and had a headache and needed to go lay down.

Nate stood up and kissed her on the cheek and asked if there was anything he could do to help her.

"No," Robin responded, "Nothing at all. I'm just very tired from so much activity today and a little nap before supper should do the trick."

As she entered the cabin through the screen door, she looked back at Nate playing with their new addition to the household. She called out to him, "Any ideas on what we should name him?"

Nate looked up from the dog towards the beauty that would be his bride, shrugged and replied, "Can we name him Jasper?"

"Yeah, I like that name," and she forced a smile, despite still feeling uncomfortable.

With Jasper finally calm and sleeping in the makeshift dog bed that Nathan had put together with an old pillow, Nathan built a fire in the fireplace, brewed some coffee, and settled in on the couch. He was secretly glad that Robin had gone in to take a nap. He needed time to think about just how he was going to let her down. She cared for him and worked very hard for the Ministry. She just didn't understand that no amount of money was going to buy into his ministry.

As he blew on the liquid inside his cup to cool it to take his first sip, Nathan was compelled to pick up his well-used Bible with the tattered cover from the pine coffee table in front of him. He held it in his hands, knowing that all the answers he was seeking were contained inside. Suddenly, he heard a voice. He recognized immediately that it was the Holy Spirit speaking to him.

He had heard the voice before, but not like this. All the times he heard the voice before, it was to direct him towards the individual he was to touch and to channel the healing power of the Lord. This time, the voice of God told him to open his bible to Corinthians 6:14.

"Do not be bound together with unbelievers; for what partnership have righteousness and lawlessness, or what fellowship has light with darkness?"

He closed his eyes. He knew that the Lord was speaking to him, but he failed to have the discernment to understand why he directed him to this scripture. He bowed his head to pray for what seemed like an eternity. The only thing that broke Nathan from his prayerful meditation was Jasper seeking his attention and Robin emerging from the bedroom.

Robin wasn't truly tired as she lay on the bed in the guestroom of Nate's cabin. She needed a sanctuary to think. Her life with Nathan had been a whirlwind. She never expected to meet a man like him, let alone fall in love. The first time he touched her in the church office at Living Waters Tabernacle, to what she had experienced just over an hour ago, convinced her that the whirlwind was unpredictable and could swirl her emotions to where she had no control.

Despite being affectionate with each other, Nathan was very old-fashioned and would not sleep with her until they were married. She wanted to be intimate right now, but she also respected Nate as a man of God, and respected his wishes to wait. She didn't want to defile any trust she had in him nor the trust he had in her, which she had worked so hard to build. Nate had placed all his faith in her for the Ministry, and this meant the world to her. Almost every aspect of how the Ministry operated was entrusted to Robin. She had power of attorney in all financial matters and if a deposit were needed into the Ministry bank account, all she had to do was ask Nate for the money. No questions asked.

If Nate had entrusted so much power in her, then why would he have to *sleep on it* regarding signing with Nashville Amusements? There weren't any downsides. Nobody would step in and try and control the Ministry. Keith Weathers made that abundantly clear. Nashville Amusements, LLC, would simply be the silent money partner. This was a win-win for Nathan Peerless Ministry.

She was his fiancé and he trusted her with *everything*! Tucking her hands behind her head, she came to the decision that this was her moment to shine in Nathan's eyes. She would be his wife soon and she knew what was best for him.

Tomorrow she would call Keith Weathers and accept his offer. The check she had in her possession would be deposited into the bank account for Nathan Peerless Ministry. She would exercise her power of attorney and sign on the dotted line to become the newest client of Nashville Amusements, LLC.

Rising from her bed, she walked out into the cabin's living room to find Nathan playing with Jasper with one hand and holding his Bible with the other.

CHAPTER 15
DECEPTION

The phone rang and Keith Weathers was hard pressed to answer it due to having a violent coughing attack. He managed to collect himself at the last ring and was able to force out a scratchy, "Hello, Keith Weathers speaking." On the other end of the line was the soon-to-be Robin Peerless.

"Good morning, Keith," she answered back, "this is Robin Gunderson from Nathan Peerless Ministry."

Keith avoided the pleasantries of idle chit chat, which neither of them appreciated, and acknowledged how good it was to hear from her. Keith listened as Robin explained how grateful she and Nathan were that Nashville Amusements would consider their ministry as a partner. Deep down Robin knew this was a lie. Nate hadn't given her his blessing at all. For a moment Keith was beginning to fear that he would hear the disappointing news that his newest target had declined his offer. This would result in the need for further persuasion from David Greene.

Then the conversation turned more positive, and Robin explained that Nathan Peerless Ministry had accepted his offer.

"Splendid," Keith exhorted! "This is better news than I have received in a long time!"

Keith asked, "When would Nathan like to sit down and meet me and my staff?"

"Oh, Nate will meet with you sometime soon, Keith, but for right now he would like me to square everything away," Robin answered.

"Very, very good, Robin," Keith replied. "My attorney will draw up our contract with all the details. Would you like me to have them send it to your attorney or directly to you?" Keith asked, hoping that an attorney wouldn't be involved.

Robin bit her lip and replied, "Have your attorney send it to *my* attention, here in Evergreen, Colorado."

Keith hung up with his newest client and took several gulps of water to clear the congestion that had formed in his throat. He felt elated. Not only would there be money to be made, lots of money, but he would indeed be meeting soon with the gifted Nathan Peerless. Then, Nathan would be touching him on his chest. He would have no choice. Soon, he would be cancer free!

CHAPTER 16
MARCHING ORDERS

Listening to the conversations between Nathan and Robin was becoming a bit tedious for David Greene. He had never been in love. He wasn't sure he had the capacity to love anybody or anything. This was his job now, to listen in, and to follow Nashville Amusements' newest prospect, at the order of Keith Weathers.

He sat with his hi-tech headphones on that allowed him to hear even the most minor noises emitting from Nathan's cabin. Rubbing his hands over his face and clean-shaven head, David reached for the bottle of Kentucky bourbon sitting next to a glass with one lone ice cube.

Pouring the bourbon into the glass, he let the liquid flow until the top of the ice was covered. He didn't drink alcohol often. He never wanted to allow his senses to be dulled to the point that he wasn't ready to spring into action at the beckoning command of his boss. Tonight was different. The discussion between Nathan and Robin alternated between business and romance. David could tolerate the business talk, but the romantic exchange truly bothered him.

The only bastion of relief David could achieve was when the bourbon started to numb his senses, or the puppy that had entered the Peerless home required their attention.

David was interrupted by his boss appearing on his computer screen. David had learned to use technology in his line of work. Despite being a man known for muscle, not brains, he did have an amazing understanding of all the techno-gizmos available. Keith got straight to the point with David as his face appeared on the computer screen.

"Good news, Peerless has signed with us. He is now our asset," Keith exclaimed! "The staff has already booked a dozen *heal-a-thon* events in the southeast. These events will be exclusive to Nathan Peerless Ministry," continued Keith.

"We don't want to muddy our brand with any outside influences at these events, do we David?" Keith asked.

David replied, "Most definitely not!"

What David heard now was exactly what he had hoped he would not hear. "David, I want you to concentrate *all* your security efforts on Nathan Peerless. He is one hundred percent your focus as of right now. Every word, every movement, you are his shadow. If he so much as burps, I want to know why," Keith explained.

Keith went on to explain that the first heal-a-thon was on December 12th in Atlanta. In just two short months Nashville Amusements would have promos, advertisements, design, and scripting complete and ready for the debut.

"Scripting," David thought to himself. "How did they get Nathan Peerless to agree to that?" What was most intriguing to David was he hadn't heard one word about this as he was spying on the couple.

Keith continued with his instructions, "David, I need you to travel to Colorado to meet with Nathan and Robin. Give them the lay of the land and make sure they're ready for Atlanta. I need to know they're on board with everything we have set up for them."

David was puzzled about one element of this journey to Colorado to meet with the mysterious Nathan Peerless. He felt he had better clarify the answers to his questions prior to confronting his newest responsibilities.

"Keith, how do I control the people who will be brought up onto the stage to be healed by Nathan Peerless?" David quizzed. "I won't know who they are or be able to vet them! This will be a security nightmare," David offered with concern.

With a little chuckle of amusement in Keith's voice, he replied to David's concerns, "David, always the consummate professional. Don't worry about our guests coming up on stage to be healed. You will have complete security clearance on each and every one! In fact, by the time we finish our third event, you will *know* each of them very well. All their ailments, inflictions, and impairments. All of which will soon be healed."

David now understood very well what Keith meant. Nathan's odds on healing these folks were about to improve greatly. Keith ended the computer session with a smile as he said, "Also, let Nathan and Robin know I will be attending the event in Atlanta!"

With that statement the computer program that projected Keith Weathers face across cyber space went dark.

David sat back in his desk chair and poured another drink. As he finished, he began to take inventory in his mind of everything he needed to pack for Colorado. He decided that one of those items he would need would be a winter coat.

CHAPTER 17
LED

Twenty Months Later

Angie Black sat, intently watching the physical therapist work on her daughter. She winced at every movement that revealed the pain that Sandy experienced from the therapy. Deep down, she felt none of this was truly helping Sandy, but this was recommended by the doctor and Angie was willing to try anything that might improve Sandy's existence.

The therapist concluded her session with Sandy and sat down to discuss the results of the therapy with the Blacks. "The scar tissue is the main issue here. It really inhibits Sandy's movement. I think with more sessions, we might be able to strengthen the muscles and tendons that support her lower spine and possibly, someday, Sandy might be able to achieve limited movement outside her wheelchair," the therapist provided her evaluation.

"How often will Sandy need to come see you for these treatments?" Angie inquired.

The therapist was typing notes on her I-Pad and without looking up to answer, replied, "I'll need to see what your insurance will allow first, but I'd like to see Sandy twice a week. Once I have an answer from your insurance, I'll call to set up a schedule."

Angie nodded her head and, after helping Sandy back into her wheelchair, rolled her out to the car. As she assisted her daughter back into the car, she couldn't help but notice the tears streaming from Sandy's eyes. She was hurting. Driving a little faster than the speed limit, Angie knew she would need to get Sandy home to the relief of the painkillers.

Once she had administered the pills, and Angie was convinced her daughter had succumbed to their relief and had settled in for a much-deserved nap, Angie walked over to her phone and called Dixie Jergens. Dixie and her husband, Ed, lived on the property just down the road from the Blacks.

They were a retired couple, with big hearts, that were always happy to help Angie and Sandy. They had been Evergreen neighbors with Angie's grandparents and were almost like family. Dixie answered the phone and after casual friendly greetings, Angie asked Dixie if she might have an hour to come up and sit with Sandy while she was sleeping. "I just need to run a quick errand, Dixie, it won't be long," Angie asked, trying not to voice the degree of desperation that she was feeling.

"Well, of course, sweetheart. This is a good time. Ed just went down for his nap," Dixie chuckled with her answer. "Where y'all need to go this time of day?" Dixie inquired without really expecting an answer.

Angie thought for just a moment. "Uhm, I just need to go to the drug store. They prescribed a new medication for Sandy, and I want to go get it right away. Supposed to help relieve the inflammation." It pained her to know she had just lied to her friend, but she wasn't prepared to reveal the truth.

Within half an hour, Dixie had arrived at the Blacks and Angie had turned the car onto the paved road that would lead to the gravel road that turned onto County Road 29 and the cabin home of Nathan Peerless.

Arriving at the driveway entrance, she put her car into park and stared down the road. She knew it was too far to see the cabin from the road and thought, for a brief moment, she might turn onto it and drive up to introduce herself to Nathan Peerless. She had no idea if he was even home although there had been murmurings around town that he was. Angie could see smoke rising in the distance that would indicate there was a fire burning in the fireplace.

She placed the car back into drive, but instead of turning onto the gravel road, Angie edged her car back onto the main road. She decided on a new destination. Evergreen Evangelical Church. As she neared the turn for the parking lot of the church, this time, she felt no apprehension. In fact, she felt like someone, or something, was pushing her to go.

Exiting the car, Angie sighted the church office door. She ascended the steps and was relieved to find the door was open. Moving into the foyer she noticed there were several offices attached, but nobody seemed to be there. She could hear footsteps coming down the hallway that led from the sanctuary to the church offices. Rounding the corner into the foyer, Pastor Mike Johnson was startled to find somebody standing there.

"Angie Black! You startled me! I didn't hear you come in. I was in the sanctuary checking the sound system. Long time, no see. How are you and Sandy doing?" Pastor Mike rambled as he extended his hand in greeting to Angie.

Angie smiled a courtesy smile back at Mike not knowing if his comment about 'long time, no see' was meant to indicate that they hadn't been to church lately. She opted to ignore the comment. "We're getting along. Sandy's still struggling with lots of pain and I'm just, let's say, doing my best to help her."

"So sorry to hear this, Angie. I'm very glad to see you though. Perhaps I can stop by your house and visit with Sandy sometime soon," Mike genuinely responded.

"Sure, that would be nice, Pastor Mike. Bring your lovely wife also," Angie added.

There was a lull in the conversation and Angie felt uncomfortable to mention what really brought her to the church today, but the silence prodded her to speak, "Pastor, I want to ask you about the healing service you're having at the church next week."

"Sure, Angie, what can I answer about it. We would love to see you, and, of course, Sandy."

Angie asked if she could sit down before she continued with her questions. Mike motioned for her to sit in a chair in the foyer and he chose the matching chair next to it. Turning toward her, he asked if he could get her a bottle of water or perhaps a Coke. "The coffee in the kitchen is probably old, but I can go brew a new pot if you'd like some."

"No, Pastor. Thank you, but I don't need anything," Angie responded in a manner that showed she had more important things on her mind.

"Go ahead, Angie, ask anything. I'm happy to answer any questions you might have," Mike encouraged Angie.

"Will Nathan Peerless be there?" Angie blurted out.

Mike was taken back by her bluntness and just a little confused by her question. "Why do you ask?" Mike quizzed.

Angie looked Pastor Mike directly in his eyes and responded, "Well, I heard he was back in town. I, uhm, understand that's what he does. He heals people."

He felt a great degree of compassion for this woman. Mike knew where the question had come from. He could see a woman hurting for her injured child. She was seeking hope. "Angie, this is the church that Nathan attends. I don't know if he'll be at the healing service. Nathan is under a court order to not organize or sponsor a healing event."

Tears began to form in Angie's eyes.

"What I do know for sure is, God will be there. The Holy Spirit will be present indeed, and if Nathan Peerless is at this meeting, God can use him, me, any of us, because he is God and no court or law can stop that," Mike responded to try and bring comfort to his guest.

After her session with Pastor Mike, and before she put the key into the car ignition, Angie thought she saw a swirling array of light above the steeple of the church. Then it dissipated, and she heard the same voice that had whispered to her in the darkness of her bedroom.

"Come. Find comfort," the voice called to her.

CHAPTER 18
BURN

Twenty months before

He could never spend enough time at his mountain home in Colorado, nor get enough rest, but Nathan knew God wanted him to get back to work and he would always listen to his God.

Winter would envelop the Colorado mountains very soon. It would bring its velvety white blanket and deposit the freshness of a different season of holidays and families gathered together. He despised traveling in the winter months unless it was to a warmer climate. The cold didn't bother him. In fact, a chill in the air brought a sense of delight to Nathan. It was the bitter freeze of winter that didn't agree with him. Still, he knew he must go where God called him. Wherever he would be needed to bring lost souls home to God.

Nate decided he would take Jasper with him on this trip. He was family now, and having him and Robin close would remind him of home. It seemed Jasper was growing twice as fast as expected and he realized that he wasn't going to be a medium-sized dog. Jasper was a bit of a runt when he picked Nate, as Martha Cook would say, but this runt of the litter was going to be a big dog!

Nathan called out from his kitchen table for Robin to come join him for coffee. The interior was a typical cabin. The kitchen cabinets were natural stained knotty pine with log walls making up the living area that led to a massive natural stone fireplace. Nathan enjoyed a fire. A real fire, in the stone fireplace, with the pine logs crackling and popping as they burned.

He called out for Robin again, this time requesting she join him to discuss business. He knew she could not and would not deny herself the opportunity to discuss the Ministry. Of course, she came into the kitchen immediately. Nathan laughed.

Robin was wearing a pair of Levi 501 jeans with a pair of black UGH boots that Nathan had purchased for her at the local Evergreen Mercantile. She had on a white, long sleeved tee shirt, covered by one of Nathan's plaid cotton shirts. He had to stop for a moment and make sure he was still breathing when she came into the kitchen. She looked gorgeous. Her hair was pulled back into a ponytail, and she had not had time to put on any makeup since getting out of the shower and getting dressed. This was the look that overwhelmed Nathan. It was simple, clean and *mountain*.

For a moment, Nathan considered taking Robin into town and to the Justice of the Peace and making her marry him today! The curves of her slender body, the softness of her skin and her angel eyes. She would soon be his and he almost couldn't wait.

Sitting down across from Nathan, she laid a folder on the kitchen table and folded her hands over the top of it. She inquired, "What's up?"

Nathan had to yank his lustful mind back to the business at hand and replied, "Okay, Ms. Personal Assistant to Nathan

Peerless, what do we have on the horizon for this Ministry? Who and where needs us?"

Nathan waited for Robin to fill him in on how she had filled their calendar but stopped himself and reached out to grasp her hands in his.

"Forgive me, love, we should pray first," Nathan insisted.

As Nathan began to pray for God to bless the Ministry, and for everything they do to glorify God, he let go of Robin's hands and jerked them back towards himself. With a panicked look on his face, he held his hands up, palms towards him, with fingers wiggling back and forth. His hands were on fire and burned with pain like he had never experienced before. They burned so bad that Nathan felt for a moment that he had touched a hot stove!

This was different than any sensation he had ever felt before. When Nathan first realized the *gift* God had bestowed on him, God would let him see who and what he would touch to bring the healing power of God. He never revealed these visions to anybody, clergy or doctor, because he believed this was a language not unlike speaking in tongues. Nathan did not have the gift to talk to God in a special language verbally, but he could see cells of cancer, a deformed spine or eyes that could not see.

When he was a young man, he would attend services and kneel to pray with somebody, grasping their hand in his. He could see what God wanted healed, and he would feel a sensation in his hands or fingers. Sometimes it was a slight tingle and then he would feel a cold sensation that gradually warmed. Once he felt the comfort of the warmth, he would reach out to touch the area of the body that was afflicted in the person.

Nathan would end the prayer once God told him he had healed the person. Nathan knew God had performed a miracle and so did the person he prayed with, and for.

This time he felt a burning sensation and the pain that accompanied it. He had no vision from God when he touched Robin, but he felt something odd, almost evil. Once the pain had subsided and Nathan's focus returned to the kitchen table, he was flabbergasted by what he saw in Robin's face. There was no recognition at all in her that something terrifying and painful had just happened to Nathan. She looked up at him and simply said, "Amen!"

Echoing her "Amen" in a stressed manner caused Robin to quiz Nathan, "Is something wrong?"

"No, no" Nathan replied, despite being confused over what had just happened. "So, what is our game plan?" Nathan asked in a somewhat dazed manner.

Robin knew this moment was inevitable and she would have to tell Nathan about her signing with Nashville Amusements, LLC. She wasn't sure how he would react, but she knew he loved her and had to trust her. Once he checked the bank account, she was sure any resentment would be gone.

Opening the folder that contained the signed contract documents was the Nathan Peerless Ministry operating plan for the next thirty-six months. Robin simply pushed the folder across the table towards Nathan.

David Greene listened intently to the conversation between Robin and Nathan. He could tell by the flipping of pages that Nathan was reading everything for the *first* time. "Holy cow," David whispered out loud, "he has no idea that she signed his ministry away!"

A voice that was usually very clear and concise was now strained and cracked. David knew it was Nathan.

"Why, why would you do this?" Nathan asked.

With a defensive tone in her voice, she responded, "Because I want more for you, Nathan. I did it for you. I did it for us."

The pain he had just endured a few moments ago was nothing compared to what he was feeling right now. He spoke in a reluctant manner to Robin, much like a father would speak to a child that had just done something wrong. "If you felt overwhelmed in planning and setting the schedule for the Ministry, then why didn't you just tell me?"

Robin replied in an objective manner, "I wasn't overwhelmed! I just felt the financial burden was prohibiting getting you out to more people, more places," there was a pause in her explanation, "and I wanted you to take me along with you."

Nathan Peerless bowed his head and closed his eyes. He spoke with his head still down, "Robin, have I ever complained about the cost of our travel? I have always provided the capital needed for the Ministry!"

Robin was becoming weary of Nathan's ignorance of how things worked. She wondered why he could not see the benefit in her plans to expand the availability of his God given talent. "Have you looked at the balance in our bank account?" she asked. "Look at it and tell me we now have enough to make our lives better."

Taken back at her statement 'make our lives better' he really didn't know how to respond to her. He thought for a moment, "What's wrong with our lives now?" Nathan had always felt it was better for Robin to not know what the cash availability of the Ministry was. Whatever she asked for, he gave her all she needed. Just like God.

Nathan responded, "I rarely look at our bank balance. There isn't much reason for me to."

"Why?" Robin quizzed. "You could give yourself a raise. You could finally have some money to afford a dishwasher and some minor luxuries for the cabin."

Nathan couldn't help but laugh a little at that last statement. He also couldn't help but feel defeated in this conversation, but Robin was his fiancé. A misguided fiancé, but his future wife, nonetheless.

Looking at the contract resting before him from Nashville Amusements, LLC, Nate saw the signing bonus amount, Nathan's annual salary and that of Robin Gundersen, Personal Assistant to Nathan Peerless. Nathan pointed to those three amounts in the documents.

"Robin, can you guess the *daily interest* I make on our Ministry account?"

"No," Robin replied.

"Well, it's more than the total of those three amounts combined," Nathan retorted.

David Greene clicked the call button with his mouse. Keith Weathers' face popped onto the computer screen. "Are you sitting down?" he asked his boss.

CHAPTER 19
HONOR

His fingers continued to tap on the manilla folder that held the fate of Nathan Peerless Ministry. Robin slouched and held her head in her hands.

"What do we do, Nate?" Robin pleaded.

"What can we do," Nathan replied.

"I thought I was doing the right thing," Robin pleaded. "I had no idea that money wasn't a problem!"

"Robin, I hate to speak to you in the manner that I am going speak to you now, but you must know that I am not only older than you in age, but I'm also older in the Lord." Nate said with an instructive look on his face. "Even if the ministry didn't have all the financial resources it could ever need or want, I know God would provide whatever we really needed. I have told you many, many, times before that our Ministry isn't about money. It's about saving people for eternity! If a person doesn't know Jesus Christ, they can't know the healing power of the Holy Spirit," Nate finished.

Much like a child that had been scolded, Robin felt the scorn of Nathan. She didn't like it, but she knew he was right. Numb to his words, she listened as Nathan explained that, as much as he didn't like the control that she had handed to

Nashville Amusements, they must abide by the contract. He could get lawyers involved, but the contract looked iron clad. He knew in his heart that the only recourse he would have is to throw the love of his life under the bus.

He wasn't prepared to do that, despite still feeling the tinge of pain he previously felt holding her hands. "This must be a ministry of integrity and honor. We, or should I say you, signed this contract and now we have no choice other than to honor it. Maybe it won't be so bad," Nathan offered, despite not seeming very confident in his words.

He scanned the contract, reading the terms that laid out the initial term of the contract that was for a period of thirty-six months. "Three long years," he cringed to himself. With that realization, Nathan heard the phone ring. The ring was obnoxious because it was a traditional push button land line. Nathan laughed at the irony that if only he had upgraded the phone to a cordless, then Robin would not have thought they were so broke.

Nathan answered the phone to discover David Greene on the other end. David didn't allude to knowing any of the trouble he had just listened in on, nor would he ever tip his hat that he had Nathan's cabin bugged. Introducing himself to Nathan as the Head of Event Security for Nashville Amusements, he asked Nate if it would be possible for him to come to Colorado to meet with him and begin the planning for their southeast tour.

Nathan, in his most gracious but strained voice, replied to David's inquiry, "Security?" Nathan had never even considered that security was necessary. "This is all new to me, but sure, David, when would you like to come?"

David had no intention of being accommodating in his timeframe to arrive in Colorado, but with all the professionalism he could muster, he responded to Nathan, "Sorry for the short notice but, actually, I'll be in Colorado tomorrow!"

"Wow," Nathan sarcastically replied, "nothing like procrastinating."

Not one for humor, David didn't offer a retort to Nathan's statement. They worked out the details of their meeting on the phone, deciding that David would come to the cabin. David was relieved that Nathan didn't offer to meet anywhere else but the cabin, because he knew he could record all the conversations. It was decided that one o'clock pm would be the meeting time.

Nathan quizzed if David needed directions from Denver International Airport to his cabin in Evergreen. David responded that he would be able to find it with GPS. Nathan thought to himself that perhaps Nashville Amusements could help them join the technology age. They wished each other well until they met tomorrow, and with parting goodbyes, David asked one last question of Nathan, "How is the weather out there, will I need a winter coat?"

Nathan responded with a question, "Where are you coming from, David?"

David replied, "Sarasota, Florida."

"Yes, you sure will," Nathan smirked. Nathan tucked the phone receiver back into the cradle and returned to sit at his kitchen table. He noticed that Jasper had decided to cozy up next to Robin's black UGH boots and he realized that you couldn't tell where the dog ended and Robin's boots began. Taking a sip of his coffee, his nose crinkled at the taste of the cold, bitter beverage.

Robin inquired, "Can I warm that coffee up for you?"

Nathan responded "Sure, that would be great."

Robin went on to ask about all the particulars of the phone call between David and Nathan. "Your boss is coming here tomorrow at one o'clock," Nate replied.

Hurt by his sarcasm, she set his coffee cup down without filling it up, turned and exited through the living room and closed her bedroom door.

Nathan knew his words had hurt her and went out onto his front porch and sat down in his favorite chair. He flung his right boot up onto the post that held up the roof over the porch. He sat there for the next three hours talking with God. After he had laid his burden at the feet of Jesus, Nate looked down to notice that Jasper had laid his at Nathan's feet.

"He sure is going to be a big dog." Nathan pondered.

In the dark of her bedroom, Robin had stopped crying an hour before she heard Nathan finish his prayers. She decided she would try praying, but she couldn't. She knew Nathan was disappointed in her actions and she would need to work twice as hard to prove her love for him. "Whatever it takes to protect him and win back his trust, I will do it," she committed to herself.

CHAPTER 20
FIRST IMPRESSIONS

A Jeep Wrangler pulled up to the front porch of the Evergreen, Colorado, world headquarters of Nathan Peerless Ministry. David Greene stepped out of the Jeep carrying a large black bag. He climbed up the five steps onto the porch and extended his hand to shake Nate's. They exchanged pleasantries then David turned his focus and attention to Robin.

"Nice to see you again, Robin," David said.

Nathan was surprised by the greeting but, before he could quiz anybody about the familiarity between Robin and David, she offered up the explanation that they had met at the initial meeting with Keith Weathers in Denver.

"Well, I guess Robin has a bit of a head start on me in lots of areas," Nathan stated. David smiled, but Robin seemed annoyed by the statement. Nathan was impressed by the physical presence exhibited by David. He presented himself in a very matter-of-fact way and Nathan appreciated that. He was slightly taller than him and no doubt hit the gym more often than Nathan ever hoped to.

Nathan was pleased that the dark sunglasses that David was wearing when he approached them came off and were placed neatly in a leather eyeglass case. Nathan needed to look into the eyes of another person and sunglasses forbade that.

The three participants in the first meeting of this *new* alliance moved off the porch and into the living room of the cabin. David spent the next three hours displaying the stage set up, access for the handicapped, lighting, music, complete with a choir and wardrobe.

Nathan's mind began to swim with the introduction of the *robe* he was to wear at the events. It was white satin with a red scarf adorned with a white embroidered cross. On the stage would be gold goblets in various sizes to administer the sacraments. Nathan stopped David right there, "Wait, whoa, hold your horses," Nathan said.

"I'm not Catholic! You can let Mr. Weathers know I am a non-denominational evangelist and wearing robes and giving communion is not how I work! If he wants that type of service, tell him to go sign the Pope!"

David smiled to the best of his ability and promised he would relay Nathan's concerns to Keith, but he already knew he would not.

Nathan thought to himself that if *Amusement* was the key word in Keith's company, then his new job was obviously as the ring announcer for this circus. He was absorbing the absurdity of it all to the best of his ability, but accepting the glitz and glamor of the stage was very hard. Then, something that David said gave Nathan a reason to pause. In the course of displaying to Nathan how people that desired to be healed would access the stage, David offered, "this access will allow a convenient and safe way for members of the audience to get to the stage thus increasing the amount of people you can heal!"

"Amount of people *I* can heal?" David replied with a questioning tone. "God heals them! I am merely a conduit for his mercy and grace. I hate to disappoint your boss, but God might not heal anybody, or he may heal many."

David chimed in based on Nathan's rebuttal and stated, "I hear what you're saying, Nathan, but it's Keith's belief that your track record is about to improve a great deal."

Not knowing exactly what David meant by his reply, Nathan looked at Robin with arms lifted in disbelief. Robin decided she could be quiet no more and interjected herself into the conversation to be a peacemaker. "What I believe David is saying, Nathan, is we are going to be very, very busy reaching more people than ever before. I pray the Lord will see fit to heal more people through you, Nathan, simply due to exposure."

Nathan shook his head in frustration and added, "I don't even need to be present for God to heal somebody. He can heal anybody who prays and believes."

Feeling out of his element to discuss this any further with Nathan, David moved on to discuss security and how he would handle it at the events. David moved through the security portion quickly as he was beginning to feel uncomfortable and, for the first time in a long time, a little intimidated by Nathan.

There wasn't any way that Nathan could stand up to him physically, but for some reason he felt uncomfortable. Keith had never sent him to set up the lay-of-the-land with anybody like Nathan before. He wanted to end this meeting, drive back to Denver, get on a plane, and call it a day. Once completing the presentation, David handed a large envelope to Nathan. As he spoke, he was sure that there might have been a slight crack of nervousness in his voice.

"Here's your sermon for every stop on the southeast tour. Keith Weathers will be there in Atlanta to greet you, along with my team," David finished.

As David turned to grab his bag after inserting his laptop into it, he reached out to shake Nathan and Robin's hands and wish them well until December.

Nathan escorted him out onto the porch, down the stairs and, as David began to climb into the rented Jeep, he waved the envelope with the sermon inside it and asked, "You said Keith Weathers will be there in Atlanta?"

"Yes, he will," David answered.

"*Can't wait,*" Nathan replied sarcastically.

CHAPTER 21
OPULENCE

Fall came and escorted winter into Evergreen, Colorado. The predictions were for a cold and snowy winter this year. There had already been a decent blizzard that had left snow drifts of eighteen feet in some areas of Colorado, but it had come and left the state just in time to get the airport in Denver open, after being closed for a few days.

Nathan appreciated just how dark Jasper's fur was because he could see him even when he got buried in the snow. Jasper loved the snow and Nathan loved to take him out to romp through it.

Robin rolled her suitcase out onto the porch and, with a couple of pats of her left hand on her hip, called Jasper to her to say goodbye. They decided not to take Jasper with them on this trip after all due to his abundant size and their whirlwind schedule that had become the *Nathan Peerless Circus* as Nate liked to call it.

A pastor friend of Nathan's from Evergreen Evangelical Church was going to stay at Nate's cabin and care for Jasper in their absence. Nathan brought a slightly snowy Jasper into the cabin, gave him a treat, and shut the cabin door behind them as they loaded their luggage and themselves into the

SUV and drove down the snow packed road and onto the plowed roadway that led to the highway and the Denver airport.

To say that their relationship had been a bit strained of late would be an understatement. Now that they were ready to embark on the three-year circus as members of the Nashville Amusements stable of stars, Nathan hoped that he and Robin could rekindle some of the spark they had before. He needed her. Especially now, because she would be all he had.

Conversation wasn't very active, or deep, between them as they journeyed down the mountain to the airport. After parking the SUV in long-term parking, they journeyed into the terminal. "What airline did our new owners book us on?" Nathan said but immediately realized that what he said was insensitive.

Robin seemed indifferent to his sarcasm. "We are going to the *private* terminal," she smugly replied. Once they had left their baggage with an attractive woman in a dark suit that looked like she was a Navy Commander, they were escorted out and boarded the plane. Nathan now knew they had entered a different realm than what he was used to. This was a private jet, with the logo of Nashville Amusements, LLC blazoned along the side. The flight crew directed Nathan and Robin to their seats, which were on opposite sides of a small square table.

There was a seat next to where Nathan was seated, but Robin felt since they were embarking on a business trip, she would sit across from the man she assisted with everything he needed. She just hoped that he would once again realize that he needed her.

The same slender woman that greeted them at the private terminal and impressed Nathan as looking like a Navy Commander came up to the couple to announce, "On behalf of Keith Weathers and Nashville Amusements, I'd like to welcome you to one of the five private jets in the NA fleet. From here forward this will be your exclusive jet, Mr. Peerless. I will always be available to you and your staff to fulfill any of your needs while you travel."

With a captivating smile, she informed Nathan that once they were underway and at cruising altitude, she would take their food and drink orders and that they could select off the menu she had placed before them. Nathan glanced at the menu of items and the first thought that entered his head was 'opulence'. He was used to fast food hamburgers, not steak and lobster. Nathan smiled back at her and requested, "Please, call me Nathan. Mr. Peerless is not necessary."

"Sorry, Mr. Peerless, but I cannot break protocol. I technically work for you now, and using your last name is, let me say, professional," the tall slender woman replied.

Robin stared at the interchange between them. She was astonished by the cadence of Nathan's speech. It bothered her slightly and made her suspicious that for the first time since she and Nathan had been in a relationship, he might be flirting. She pushed it from her mind and simply smiled.

Shortly after being airborne, Robin opted to break the silence between them and asked, "Have you read the sermon they wrote for you?"

"Yes, yes I have," Nathan responded.

"Will you give the sermon they wrote for you, Nathan?" she inquired.

"I can't," Nathan replied.

"Good," Robin added as she stared out of the jet window at the vastness of sky that surrounded it.

Nathan grabbed Robin's hand in his and held it tight. This time, Nathan did not feel anything odd. He didn't feel a burn or a coldness. In a way he was grateful it was normal. Robin felt hope when Nathan touched her. She had not felt hope since she had betrayed his trust. She fell asleep for the first time in days.

CHAPTER 22
EMBARK

The lights were on inside the auditorium that would host the first Nathan Peerless Ministry Tour Event. Nathan was impressed, noting that a church, even a mega-church, could not have an auditorium this large. How could they possibly fill this auditorium?

Robin wondered how many seats this auditorium had. She told Nate she guessed it was approximately eight thousand.

"Eight thousand?" Nate gasped! Why would Nashville Amusements book this large of a venue for him? The revival in Memphis had three thousand and that was the largest crowd he had ever seen.

The auditorium was a gorgeous sight to see. The stage was huge and adorned with beautiful potted flowers of every varietal. A huge projected screen behind the pulpit appeared to be at least fifty feet in height and one hundred feet across. The sound system was being tested as Nathan and Robin walked up the ramp that they assumed was for wheelchair access. There was a landing area for wheelchairs at the top that Nathan believed would allow almost 100 wheelchairs to be positioned. Huge digital monitors all over the auditorium at every exit read:

Nathan Peerless Ministry
Presented by Nashville Amusements

On the digital readouts were pictures of Nathan holding out his hand as if beckoning those in need of healing to come to him.

"Odd," Nathan thought to himself, "I don't remember ever posing for that picture and I've never put on that ridiculous robe." As Nathan stood in awe of the spectacle before him, a voice sounded through the speaker system.

"Inspiring, isn't it, Nathan?" the voice asked.

Robin came to stand by Nathan as they both pivoted to see where the voice might be coming from. Keith Weathers walked from the audio/visual center at the back of the auditorium down the aisle that led up onto the stage. Robin was the first to greet Keith as she was closest to him, and Keith extended both his hands to her in greeting.

"So nice to see you again, Robin," Keith remarked like seeing a long-lost friend.

Robin didn't recall his hands being so cold the last time they met. Keith let go of Robin's hands and extended his hand out to shake Nathan's. "What an honor it is to finally get to meet the *star* of our show, the *infamous* Nathan Peerless," Keith offered.

"Yes, good to meet you also, Mr. Weathers," Nathan replied.

Keith retorted, "Oh, please, call me Keith, Nathan, Mr. Weathers was my father."

"Okay, *Mr. Weathers*," Nathan replied with a bit of sarcasm in his voice.

Keith didn't seem to pick up on Nathan's sarcastic reply, but Robin certainly did. She was glad that Keith was preoccupied with reveling in *his* production. Robin thought just how much thinner and gaunt Keith looked since their meeting in Denver. She hoped he wasn't ill.

It seemed like a page out of a theatrical play, but Nathan couldn't help but notice just how much Keith looked like his stepfather. Maybe not as tall, but certainly his features resembled the man that came to raise him. It was hard to separate the feelings he had for his stepfather, whom he didn't have many fond memories of, and this man that he only just met. It made Nathan feel uncomfortable and he did his best to try and focus on the meeting at hand.

Keith went on to review with his newest asset just how spectacular this event would be. David Greene walked out from behind the screen to greet Keith, Robin, and Nathan on the stage.

"Ah, David, welcome," Keith exclaimed. "So good of you to join us.

David, do you have any additional information you need to provide to Nathan and Robin regarding security for the event tonight?"

David responded, "No, just rest assured, we'll have their backs every moment."

Nathan was confused by David's reply to Keith's question. This was an evangelical event. "Protection for me?" he pondered. "What is this world coming to?"

"Well then," Keith remarked, "if there are no other concerns, I will excuse myself to get ready for tonight and this magnificent journey we have embarked upon together."

Nathan turned towards Keith as he was preparing to depart to ask a question, "Mr. Weathers, this is a large auditorium, and I was just curious why we booked such a large venue for tonight? I mean, this being the first *show* and all."

Keith laughed as he continued to walk down the ramp to exit the auditorium. He answered as he continued to walk away, seeming to truly enjoy the question. "Mr. Peerless," he chuckled as he responded, "this is a ten thousand seat auditorium. This event has been *sold out* for weeks!"

CHAPTER 23
FISHING

He could hear the sound increase over the loudspeakers. Music began to play, and the Nathan Peerless Ministry choir began to sing. He wasn't sure he had ever heard a better sounding choir. These voices were professional with every harmonic chorus they sang.

Nathan was nervous. He couldn't remember ever being this nervous before and Robin could sense just how tense he was. "I'll be right here waiting for you," she said as she looked into Nathan's eyes. He gave her a kiss on the cheek and looked down at the white satin robe with the crimson scarf he was wearing and couldn't help but wonder just how stupid he looked.

"The robe is coming off," he said as he hurriedly pulled it over his head. Robin picked it up from the backstage floor and attempted to try and fold it. Then he heard the announcement on the overhead speaker.

Brothers and sisters, the time has come to witness a man that has the touch of God. Without further delay, please give a warm kingdom welcome to Brother Nathan Peerless!

In blue jeans and a Denver Broncos tee shirt Nathan walked out onto the stage with a wave of one hand and his bible in his other. He wished he had worn his old Nacona boots rather than his Nike tennis shoes. Both were comfortable footwear, but he felt the tennis shoes projected an image of being a college student, which he clearly was not.

Sitting in a private booth high up in the most obscure area of the church auditorium, Keith almost choked when Nathan came out onto stage, *without* the robe. "That's great," he thought, "no robe! That robe cost $2,300 dollars!" Still, the crowd went crazy with enthusiasm at the sight of Nathan.

Staring at the light show that beamed its dance upon the stage at his appearance, Nathan felt the nervousness he had experienced backstage suddenly leave. Being here, on stage, with the opportunity to preach the word of God, to give his audience that might not know Jesus the opportunity to get to know him, this was his natural element. This is where God wanted him.

Before the light show ended and the spotlight would come to focus on him, Nathan had a sudden memory come to him. A memory of his stepfather. He remembered the first Sunday after God healed his friend and benefactor, Paul Merrifield. He had been so eager to attend church that day. His eagerness had resulted in him receiving very little sleep the night before.

It wasn't the accolades he might receive or the recognition of his *gift* from his friends and neighbors that would be attending the services that morning, he wanted to be a witness to any person attending that day that had come seeking the Lord. He could speak, even as a young man, with conviction, about the meaning of Salvation. He thought; what better way to reach people than on the heels of the miracle that God worked through him, with Paul.

The memory revealed that he never got the chance to go to church on that Sunday. His stepfather swung open Nathan's bedroom door and barged in, calling out like a banty rooster, "C'mon boy, get yor sorry butt out of bed and get yor fishin clothes on. We be going fishin this mornin."

Nathan was in no mood to go fishing that morning. He had other plans, but as he watched his stepfather pull a small flask of moonshine whiskey out of his pocket, unscrew the cap, and guzzle the liquid inside, Nathan knew his refusal to go fishing would not be accepted. Still, with all the boldness he could muster, he knew he must try. "I would love to go fishin with you today, but I need to be in Church this mornin, Pops."

Pops, which was the name Nathan called his stepfather by, looked at him with the scorn of a Pharisee pronouncing Jesus as a blasphemer. "Enough of this religious crap, boy. I've heard enough about you from all the townsfolk this week. You need to get away from all that church stuff for a while! Get yor'n gear and meet me at the truck in ten minutes."

At the lake, Nathan placed a worm on the hook and checked to make sure his red and white bobber, that would hold the worm from sinking to the bottom, was tightly secured to the fishing line. Just as he held the line in one hand and prepared to give it and his baited rig a toss out into the water, Nathan caught a glimpse of his stepfather lying on the ground.

Nathan dropped his pole and ran over to where his stepfather had dropped to the ground. He stood over him with the realization that something had occurred to cause his stepfather to lose consciousness and fall to the ground. Nathan stood motionless. Unlike with Paul, he heard no command from God to reach down and touch his Pops. He would not be called to provide the conduit of healing with his touch.

Not today.

As quickly as the memory arrived, it vanished. Nathan wasn't sure why the death of his stepfather entered his mind, especially at this moment, but he brought his attention back to delivering the Lord's message to those who needed to hear it. Robin sat off stage and wondered just how upset everybody from Nashville Amusements was getting, because Nathan wasn't following the script. He preached to the audience, not a sermon that had been provided for him, but from his heart. When he had completed the message, he ended with the invitation he had always offered to those that attended one of his services. He invited all to come forward and learn about living a life with Christ as your savior.

This invitation was different. Nathan began to see thousands coming forward, towards the stage. They were coming in wheelchairs, and with crutches, and some were being carried. They were coming forward for one thing, and one thing only, and that was to receive the *touch* of Nathan Peerless. For the next three hours, Nathan bowed and prayed with as many people as he could.

As he did, it occurred to him that God had not showed him any afflictions. He hadn't felt a cool sensation in his fingers that turned to warmth. Not once did God tell him to *heal!* Despite not having his usual sessions with the Lord, several people attending claimed to be healed. A few of the people that were wheelchair bound stood up from their seats and walked away from the stage to the crying and weeping of the people around them. It did not feel right to him. It did not feel right at all.

When the event was over, and Nathan lay exhausted on a sofa in his dressing room, Robin sat in a chair across from him. She had a troubled look on her face.

David Greene walked into the dressing room and grabbed a bottle of water off the table of refreshments and snacks reserved for the event staff and performers. He stood at the doorway threshold as if he were expecting somebody to enter momentarily. Keith Weathers strolled in a few moments later.

"Nicely done, Nathan," Keith remarked like a coach that brought his team on a comeback to win the game. "Mission accomplished, despite the fact you didn't exactly follow orders," Keith added.

Nathan lifted his weary head to look at Keith. "Sorry boss, I just couldn't give the sermon that was provided," Nathan replied.

Keith retorted to Nathan's statement, "Was it not good enough? Perhaps it was too corny or sappy?"

Nathan said "Oh, not at all. In fact, it was a little too good. The audience would have recognized that it wasn't from me!"

Keith projected a broad smile and replied, "I appreciate that response, Nathan. I wrote that sermon. Always the writer and never the singer." Keith laughed. "Nathan", Keith asked in a very calm and almost friendly manner, "would you do me a favor in exchange for me never making you wear the robes again? Oh, and I also agree to remove the beautiful chalices and adornments from the stage," he added.

"What can I do for you, boss?" Nathan quizzed, feeling that an agreement was pending that might be mutually beneficial.

Keith replied as he glanced at Robin and David Greene, "Would you kneel with me and pray?"

Nathan was a bit surprised by Keith's request and, despite being exhausted and physically spent from the events of that night, Nathan motioned for Keith to kneel beside him. "How can I pray for you tonight?" Nathan asked.

"Pray for healing, Nathan, simply pray for healing," Keith replied.

Just before Nathan closed his eyes to pray, he saw a look of concern on David's face and even that of Robin's.

He reached out and put his arm around Keith's shoulder and began to pray. For the first time that night, the Lord showed Nathan a sickness. Nathan knew immediately it was cancer. He had seen it before. Nathan waited for the Lord to guide him through the special journey of healing that he had done so many times before. Nathan was prepared to listen to the special language that God spoke to him. He was prepared to listen to God. He was prepared to feel the coolness in his fingers and as the warmth of God's healing powers surfaced, he would touch the cancer and Keith Weathers would be healed.

Nathan did not feel the warmth this time, but God did speak to him. God spoke, "This man does not know me. His heart is hardened towards me. His illness must remain." Nathan ended his verbal prayer and released his arm from Keith's shoulder.

"Is it done," Keith eagerly asked. "You must know?"

Robin looked on with a blank stare on her face. Nathan looked up towards her with a sad look upon his face and said "No, Keith, I was too weak. I did not have enough faith tonight."

Keith rose to his feet, although it did not seem like it came without a struggle. "Well, Nathan, now you, and you alone, know my darkest secrets. We'll have many, many more opportunities to accomplish what we need to do."

Nathan nodded his head to affirm Keith's desire. Keith turned and walked out of Nathan's dressing room. David turned to follow his boss out the door but, before exiting, said to Robin, "Tell healer boy here he did real good tonight! At fifty-six dollars a pop, we'll make our money back in no time!"

After Keith and David had left, Robin turned her attention to Nathan. Nathan, even more exhausted, had returned to reclining on the couch. Robin grabbed his head affectionately and cupped it in her hands. "My dear Nathan, what have I done? What have I gotten you into?"

Nathan did not respond to her. He understood now, why God had placed the memory of his stepfather's death in his mind. He didn't understand it then, but he did now. His touch could be used to heal if God anointed it. His touch could be used to bring healing, and with it, Salvation to those who were healed. God knew those that would receive his word and would become his children. God was in control, and he was a God of second chances. Nathan knew that his stepfather had run out of chances, but he had been brought here to offer that second chance. To Keith Weathers.

CHAPTER 24
THE SPIRIT

Nathan's attitude towards Keith Weathers had changed. Every moment that he had to converse and witness to Keith, he cherished. Every one of those moments he had with Keith was an opportunity to share the word of God and bring true salvation to Keith. Although his boss seemed to understand the pathway to salvation, and even recited scripture back to Nathan, God would show the cancer in Keith growing and consuming his mortal body.

Keith continued to ask for healing with every event that Nathan did. Each time, Nathan did not hear the voice of God saying it was time to heal Keith. In fact, with every event that Nathan performed, the voice of God was absent. He was confused as to why so many that came forward for the healing touch from God seemed to actually be healed.

Then the answer came to him. He felt so naïve to have not known the answer. It finally occurred to him after finishing an event in Mobile, Alabama. A seeker for healing came in his wheelchair and waited patiently to move forward in his place in line. When the man made it up to Nathan, something seemed amiss to him. He stood back for a moment and stared intently at the wheelchair bound man.

The man smiled at Nathan with an eerie grin. A facial gesture that Nathan recognized from his event in Atlanta, Georgia. This same man had come up on that stage in a wheelchair there also and walked off that stage on his own. Reaching out to this same man, Nathan felt and heard nothing, but the man suddenly rose from his wheelchair.

Nathan felt disgusted and betrayed. This wasn't a miracle from God. This man was a *plant*. With every call of hallelujah that reverberated from those around the man and out in the audience, Nathan felt more and more sick to his stomach.

He abruptly ended the event, much to the dismay of the crowd and those frauds waiting for their fake healing and a paycheck from Nashville Amusements. Once Nathan exited the stage and had entered his dressing room, he collapsed on the velvet covered sofa that traveled with him to each event, and each city.

Keith knocked softly on the door of his dressing room, not to gain permission to enter, but instead to alert Nathan of his arrival. He was followed by Robin and David into the dressing room.

"Are you okay, Nathan?" Keith called out as if he was truly concerned.

Nathan lifted his head, which had been nestled into his chest, and in an angry manner demanded that Robin and David leave the dressing room, leaving him and Keith alone. David seemed perturbed at the demand, but Keith held out his arms with hands extended palms first at David. With a motion that indicated he would be alright, David and Robin exited.

Outside the dressing room, Robin was the first to speak about what just happened. "What's that all about?" she quizzed.

"I think our healer boy just caught on to the con and isn't happy about it," David replied.

"Con? What con?" Robin asked in an earnest and confused manner.

Keith gathered a folding chair, opened it and sat directly at eye level with Nathan. "I see you're disturbed by something. I don't like to see any of my stars, let's just say, disturbed."

"Star? Is that what I am? Well, let me tell you something, Mr. Weathers, I'm no star! God is the star. I'm nothing more than a fraud," Nathan bellowed as a debate captain in a rebuttal.

"You're no fraud, Nathan, I've seen the miracles. I believe in them. I believe there are more to come. I believe there is still one for me," Keith retorted attempting to gain control of the conversation by flattery.

Nathan sat up from the slouched position he was in on the sofa and, with an intense expression, addressed Keith. "Let me ask you a question. If you believe in me so much, why all the fake people seeking healing?"

There was a delay in the answer. A heavy sigh from Keith preceded the answer. "Nathan, first and foremost, I'm a businessman. The more people the public see healed, the more tickets we sell."

"So, you don't truly believe God can heal people? You need to set up a farce, a scam, and it's only to make money?" Nathan questioned Keith, knowing full well what the answer was going to be.

Keith stood up from his chair and paced the room. Without looking at Nathan, he spoke, "Nathan, I believe that *you* can heal people with a gift from God, one of the spiritual gifts as described in 1 Corinthians 12 verse 7-11. Let me see…the scripture goes something like this. *Now to each one the manifestation of the Spirit is given for the common good. ⁸ To one there is given through the Spirit a message of wisdom, to another a message of knowledge by means of the same Spirit, ⁹ to another faith by the same Spirit, to another gifts of healing by that one Spirit, ¹⁰ to another miraculous powers, to another prophecy, to another distinguishing between spirits, to another speaking in different kinds of tongues,ʲ and to still another the interpretation of tongues. All these are the work of one and the same Spirit, and he distributes them to each one, just as he determines.*"

"Very good, Keith. You've memorized a very important scripture in the New Testament. I'm impressed," Nathan responded.

Keith smiled.

"Still, do you understand who that one Spirit is? Because every time you come to me to heal your disease, I question if you truly understand," Nathan quizzed as a Sunday School teacher might.

Keith didn't respond to Nathan's inquiry.

"I know why you used Robin to get to me. It wasn't the money you could've made. It wasn't the new toy for promotion. It wasn't that you wanted to be first in the game. You knew I didn't need your money," Nathan continued.

"Yes, you are correct, my dear Nathan. You have more money than I could ever hope to have. It's my job to get to know where my targets are vulnerable. I knew all about your inheritance of the Merrifield estate. In many ways, I'm envious of you and I'm envious of him. He received your touch and was provided a second chance," Keith admitted.

"Then you also understood that Robin was where I was vulnerable," Nathan responded.

With no acknowledgement of the truth being revealed, Keith had no reason to confirm it. "Perhaps you're right. I don't know the Spirit that you do. I just know that you can heal me. That was my motivation for all of this. The show, the production, is nothing more than fluff."

Once he had concluded his statement, Nathan witnessed a glassy eyed look come on to Keith's face. His skin turned ashen and drops of blood appeared from his nose. Then, without warning, he dropped to his knees and collapsed on the floor.

Nathan dropped beside Keith and reached out to try and revive consciousness but was unsuccessful. With a loud shout, Nathan called out for anybody that might be within earshot to come and assist him. David Greene was the first to enter through the door followed by Robin directly behind him.

David approached Keith in a panicked manner and reached down to take his pulse. With irritation evident in his voice, he almost scolded Nathan. "What did you do to him? What happened?"

Nathan responded with a great deal of restraint, despite his disdain for David's attitude. "He's alive, you need to call for an ambulance, and I do mean immediately!" David complied with the request and within a few minutes, paramedics arrived and took Keith to a local hospital.

Once Keith had left in the ambulance accompanied by David Greene, Robin came to the sofa where Nathan was and sat beside him. With a solemn look on her face, she couldn't help but bring up the inevitable subject that was now clear to her. "Keith's sick, isn't he?"

Nathan nodded.

"Has he been asking for you to heal him?" Robin questioned.

Nathan nodded.

"You can't, can you?"

"No, I can't."

CHAPTER 25
DECISIONS

It was very clear to Nathan that the focus of Nathan Peerless Ministry events was not to bring God's message to all who needed it. At fifty-six dollars a ticket, he was going to be a money-making machine for Nashville Amusements, LLC!

Nobody but Nathan knew the conversation or what happened in the dressing room in Mobile, between Keith and him. Nathan couldn't possibly explain to anybody, even if he wanted to, that when he bent down to assist a collapsed Keith Weathers, he experienced a sensation he had never experienced before. It wasn't the voice of God speaking to him, instructing him, instead, he had been plunged into darkness and felt nothing but despair.

There wasn't light, or hope, and he felt evil, in its purest sense, all around him.

Keith had been admitted into the hospital and was recovering to the extent that his doctors believed he could be released soon, but with very strict restrictions. His schedule of running Nashville Amusements on a day-to-day basis was out of the question. Fortunately, reports of his disease were being treated with the greatest amount of discretion. Probably thanks to Robin Gunderson and David Greene.

Nathan began to experience a descent into deep depression. Each event that he did on the southeast tour presented the same scenario. Thousands would come forward on Nathan's invitation, and thousands would be divinely healed. With the thousands that came to Nathan, he had no communication with God, but thousands professed to be healed. He began to understand who and what these people were. They were just *plants* and on the payroll of Keith Weathers.

He was sickened every time he went on stage. Where Keith's cancer was concerned, God no longer showed it to Nathan. He felt alone and sad. Not because he was no longer receiving the precious gift from God, but mostly because he was slowly not talking to God at all. Prayer had ceased because he was embarrassed.

The only person who seemed to be thriving in this environment of events and amusements was Robin Gundersen. It was evident to Nathan that she had Keith Weathers' ear, and despite suspecting Nathan's growing discontent, she pushed him into longer healing services, even though she knew he wasn't truly healing anybody.

Nathan couldn't recall the last time he had been the instrument of the Holy God and felt the joy of bringing a soul to Jesus.

The southeast tour turned into the northeast tour which turned into the mid-America tour. Nathan's fame multiplied. On a day that Nathan was experiencing a rare break from the grueling tour schedule, Robin approached Nathan as he read his bible while drinking his coffee.

"We got an offer to do a television documentary special!" Robin blurted out.

"Television," Nathan reverberated with an astonished attitude.

Robin explained that Keith had been approached by a major cable network to do a documentary series on Nathan and to broadcast his healing events to the nation. "Keith is excited about this next step in your career," Robin offered like a mother offering to take a kid for ice cream.

Nathan couldn't seem to conjure a response of either interest or disdain.

"His health is failing rapidly and, quite frankly, *we* don't understand why you won't heal him. We know that you can! Keith is on borrowed time and if the media finds out that you refuse to heal him, your reputation could be tarnished and opportunities like television would go away!" she pleaded.

Nathan no longer saw the beauty in Robin that he once was held captive by. The feelings he once had for this woman were fading and, perhaps, might be gone. "Robin," Nathan took a deep breath before saying anything else, "I'm going back to Colorado. I've made the decision that these last eighteen months I've had to endure are long enough. I want to see Jasper, and fall is coming soon to *my* mountain home," Nathan said with a resolve that couldn't be questioned or argued.

Robin, with a questioning attitude, asked, "Don't you mean *our* mountain home?"

He knew the moment had come to be honest with her and revealed to her the decision his heart had made. He told her that he had not healed anybody or been any part of God's plan to heal people since she joined them to Keith Weathers and Nashville Amusements. He told her that he was breaking the contract and going home. Then, the portion of his decision that he had most dreaded was revealed. She was not part of his plans.

"I don't know what the future holds for you, Robin, but it isn't being with me. I'm going home alone. I need to seek God, and I must do that by myself!" Nathan exclaimed.

Robin did not say a word. She turned and walked out of their hotel suite in Kansas City. Nathan felt lost and wondered if all this had made him a hardened and cruel man. He packed his bag and called for a cab to take him to the airport where he would take the first flight out to Denver, Colorado.

As Nathan rode in the cab to the airport, his heart felt empty. Not just for love lost between Robin and himself, but had all this caused him to lose his God? Perhaps even worse, maybe God didn't love him anymore.

CHAPTER 26
DOUBT

Sandy was emphatic that her mother let her go with her friends to a local church league softball game. Deep down, Angie had a nagging intuition about letting her daughter ride in a car with a relatively young and new driver. She felt that wasn't something she should agree to.

"Geesh, mother, Jennifer's a good driver. Her mom trusts her, and the softball fields aren't very far. Evergreen Evangelical is playing Timberline Pentecostal and it's for the chance to go to the championship game! Afterward, we're all going back to the church to hopefully celebrate," her young teenage daughter pleaded with great zeal and persuasion.

Angie knew that Sandy couldn't care less about softball or sports. Her interest was in the second baseman, Josh. To say that she was overprotective of her daughter would be an understatement. She tried her best to give her little freedoms here and there, if only to try and alleviate her own self-doubt that Sandy would make the same poor decisions that she had.

"Please, mom," Sandy reiterated several times repeatedly.

Although that nagging sensation hadn't left her, Angie agreed to let Sandy go. She hugged her mother with affectionate gratitude, which made the decision a little easier.

After the girls, Sandy and Jennifer, and another friend, Tori, left to embark on their outing, Angie sat alone in her modest farmhouse home.

The quiet and loneliness crept in, but more importantly, the realization that someday in the very near future she would be alone. No daughter would be there to tend to her daily needs, and this was a feeling that disturbed Angie. She was glad that she had started to attend Evergreen Evangelical with Sandy. Relationship choices could have been a lot worse for her and Sandy. The people that attended the church were friendly and kind, but she hadn't quite captured the love of Jesus like many had professed.

He knew he had drunk too many beers, and the two shots of whiskey had helped to enhance his inebriation. As he tried to place the key into the ignition, he fumbled for the keys, and they fell to the floor of his truck. Once his hand had trolled to find the keys on the floor, he felt dizzy and thought for a moment he might just lay down on the seat and take a nap.

As he started the truck and pulled out of the gravel parking lot of Evergreen Tavern, he entered the paved roadway. He understood he must get home as his wife had planned a family get-together and to be late would have ensured he would be in the doghouse. Off to his right were softball fields and he could see the lights beginning to illuminate due to dusk having come to this mountain town.

Noticing the players playing catch reminded him of his younger days. He loved to play ball and had been a good player in his younger days. He looked in the rearview mirror at his now older and wrinkled face and smiled. His gaze into the rearview mirror had caused him to veer the truck over the medium and into oncoming traffic.

The phone rang, jolting Angie from the peace she was experiencing with the absence of her daughter. After a short conversation, she abruptly placed the phone receiver back in the cradle of the old-fashioned land line phone, and with panicked urgency, bolted out her door and was on her way to Evergreen Memorial Hospital. Driving as fast as she could, totally ignorant of the speed limit or her safety, she felt tears of remorse dripping down her face. Her thoughts couldn't help but explore that what had happened was that God was punishing her.

At the funeral of Sandy's friends, Jennifer and Tori, Angie did her best to console the families of these girls. Sandy was still in critical condition, but despite the best efforts of the emergency doctors at Evergreen Memorial, the decision was made that her daughter would need advanced care, and she was air flighted to a hospital in Denver.

Many of the people that were attending the funeral came to offer prayers and hope to Angie for Sandy's recovery. After the funeral was over, she packed her suitcase and headed to Denver. Angie had to be with her daughter every waking moment. Several months later, Sandy was moved to a rehabilitation hospital to begin therapy to minimize the pain and provide occupational therapy to make her mobile in a wheelchair.

Sandy's doctors provided no hope that Sandy would ever be able to walk again. Angie was relieved that the wounds on Sandy's face and skull, from being hurled through the front windshield of the car she was riding in on that fateful evening, had begun to heal and minimize with only slight scarring. If she wouldn't walk again, at least she would still have her beauty.

Once Sandy had been released from the rehabilitation center, they returned to their home in Evergreen. Angie was happy to be home, but she also understood the road forward would be paved with many obstacles.

Angie sat on the side of Sandy's bed and reassured her daughter that she would always be there for her. The pain, both physical and mental, was omnipresent with Sandy. Out of the blue, Sandy asked her mother, "Was the funeral nice?"

"Yes, very nice. Lots of people came."

"Was it held at the church?" Sandy nonchalantly asked.

Angie, without understanding the direction this conversation was heading, but having no intuition that it was anything other than chit-chat, answered, "Yep."

Sandy looked at her mother and replied with a statement that Angie could tell had come with thought and consideration by her daughter, "I don't ever want to go back to church."

CHAPTER 27
A BATTLE JUST BEGUN

Arriving at the airport, Nathan, without thinking, told the taxi driver to take him to the private terminal. Catching his error before it was too late, he winced at the thought that he had become so conditioned to the *star* lifestyle he had been living. Quickly instructing the driver to chart a new direction and take him to the main terminal, Nathan grabbed his bag and proceeded into the terminal to try and catch the next commercial flight out to Denver International Airport.

He looked carefully at all the airlines that had flights going to Denver when suddenly he had a change of heart. God was telling him that it was fine to retreat to his home in Evergreen, but first he had to do the right thing and confront Keith Weathers, in person. Nathan found a flight that was bound for Nashville, and it was scheduled to depart in a couple of hours. Discovering that the flight only had one seat available, Nathan was aware that he was following what God needed him to do.

During the flight to Nashville, it occurred to Nathan that once he landed, he had no idea what the address was for Nashville Amusements or if Keith would even be there. Afterall, the last time he saw Keith, he watched him being carted off in an ambulance. Although he was experiencing some anxiety about whether this excursion was going to be a failure if Keith wasn't available, still, something tugged at his belief that this was something God wanted him to do or at least try.

Walking into the main terminal and out to public transportation, Nathan got his answer. Standing by a black SUV with the passenger door wide open was none other than David Greene.

"Hello, David. You seem to have a better idea where in the world I am than God does," Nathan delivered his greeting in his usual sarcastic tone.

"Welcome to Nashville, Healer Boy. Keith is expecting you," David replied as Nathan entered the vehicle.

Having never been to the Corporate Headquarters of Nashville Amusements, Nathan was impressed by the opulence of the building. He displayed no surprise in his expression. Not because he didn't want David to see any amazement in his reaction, but mainly because he truly wasn't surprised. The building and its surroundings were, to say the least, expected.

David called on his radio as they approached the front entrance alerting Keith that his *asset* had arrived.

"Very good, send him up to my penthouse. He is fine to come alone, David," Keith's voice responded.

"Copy that, boss," David replied.

The elevator door opened to reveal a darkened room. Nathan could tell that the music played in the elevator was Keith's hit song being sung by his star, Cole. As he carefully navigated his way into the room, he heard a voice call out from behind a doorway that was partially ajar. Gingerly moving through the open door, Nathan found another adjacent room that, despite being dark like the room he had just passed through, was better lit and Nathan could clearly tell this room was a recording studio.

Sitting on a black stool and holding an acoustical guitar on his lap was a frail and pale man. If Nathan hadn't known Keith before, he might have questioned if this was the same man. Waving Nathan over to where he was sitting, Keith patted his hand on a chair sitting next to him.

Nathan obliged the offer.

Keith began to play the riff of *Pull Up a Rock and Fish Awhile.*

When Keith began to sing the lyrics, although the opulence of this building didn't surprise him, Keith's voice certainly did. Nathan had never proclaimed himself to have a good singing voice. God hadn't blessed him with that gift. Despite the sickly appearance of the man passionately singing the vocals to this song, he could undeniably carry a tune.

Halfway through the song, Keith stopped and placed his guitar on the floor. Unable to continue because of a violent coughing attack, Keith did his best to be polite and conceal the pain he was clearly experiencing. Nathan saw a pitcher of water and a glass sitting on a small table, and pouring some water into the glass, handed it to Keith. Once he had regained his composure, Keith thanked Nathan for fetching it for him.

With a glance that seemed far off in the distance, Keith spoke. "You know that song I was singing built everything you see here."

"I'm aware. Good song," Nathan replied.

"No, it's a great song," Keith smiled as he answered.

"How did you know I would come here," Nathan, tired of idle chit-chat, asked.

"It's my job, dear man. No, it's my duty to the entire company to know exactly what my family is doing and where they're at. I still consider you part of the family, Nathan."

"That's why I came, Keith. I need to go home. I'm finished with this scam. What do you need from me to walk away?" Nathan pleaded.

"And Robin? Is she also finished with our little venture?"

"I can't answer for Robin. My guess is she isn't. I've been replaced with another idol."

Keith said nothing in rebuttal, but Nathan could see the affirmation to what he had just said in his eyes.

"I need your touch. I need to be free from this disease. That's my price. There, you asked, and I've answered," Keith revealed bluntly.

Nathan stood from his stool and slowly paced about the room. "Have you come to Jesus? Have you resigned yourself to the understanding that it is our Lord that can heal you?"

"I believe that you can heal me," Keith proclaimed.

"Then I have failed you. I'm not worthy and my words have not penetrated your heart and mind to reveal the truth."

"If you walk away now, Mr. Peerless, without satisfying the terms of our contract, I will ruin you and your reputation. I have a great many contacts that will portray me as the victim here. Everything you have accomplished, and everything you've done in the past will expose you as nothing more than a fraud," Keith's voice suddenly seemed different, and evil.

Nathan walked to the door that led to the darkened room that would provide him with access to the elevator. Whatever God had hoped to have him accomplish here today was obviously in vain. As he reached the door, Nathan called out to Keith, "I love you, Keith. More importantly, God loves you."

It would take Nathan three hours to walk from Corporate Headquarters to somewhere where he could get a taxi to return to the airport. Upon reaching the ground level and entrance of the building, he confirmed that David was gone. He was grateful for the time, and the walk, to reflect and search his soul.

David walked into the recording studio to find his boss strumming his guitar in quiet contemplation. "What now, Keith? Shall I go into recovery mode?" David inquired.

"Not this time, David. I have another plan. A more subtle plan. Call Robin and tell her I need her to come to Nashville immediately."

"Copy that, boss," David responded.

As David departed to carry out the orders, Keith returned to singing his song with his eyes closed in subtle submission to a battle that had only just begun.

CHAPTER 28
TREASURE

Nathan pulled into his gravel driveway in Evergreen twenty hours after leaving Robin, Nashville Amusements, Keith Weathers and fake healings. Jasper came running out to see him as if they had never been apart. Despite a couple of phone visits in the last eighteen months, Nathan had not been home to where he belonged.

Pastor Mike from Evergreen Evangelical Church sat with Nathan on his porch sipping one of his extra strong brews of coffee. Nathan appreciated Mike more than he could say. He had been a true blessing through his troubled eighteen months. Long telephone conversations with Mike had helped him to see that what he was living was not God's plan.

Nathan filled Mike in on what brought him to the decision to break the contract with NA, and the woman he thought he loved, Robin. His gift was gone, and with it, his love for Robin.

"Nathan, do you think you'll need to get a lawyer?" Mike asked.

"Well, I am breaking a contract, even though Robin signed it," Nathan replied.

Mike continued to explain that it wasn't the breach of contract that Nathan should be worried about. He explained he should be more concerned about being charged with fraud.

"Fraud?" Nathan blurted and questioned with surprise.

"How can I be charged with fraud?"

"Obviously you haven't watched any television lately," Mike explained in a tongue in cheek manner. "A news report from a Denver station talked about an Evergreen man who has been allegedly passing himself off as a faith healer. The report went on to say that he would charge people an exorbitant rate to attend events with the promise of healing them, but he never really healed anybody at all."

He told Nathan that the President and CEO of Nashville Amusements has filed claim with the Tennessee Attorney General claiming that he even duped him into paying large amounts of cash with the promise of curing him of his stage 4 lung cancer. "He's asking for a Grand Jury to render indictments against him."

Nathan's heart sunk and for the first time in his life he understood the saying 'hell hath no fury like a woman scorned'! He also learned just how evil Keith Weathers was and why his possibility of ever being healed of lung cancer was as distant as his relationship with God.

Mike explained to Nathan that prior to finding Jesus and becoming a pastor, he was in the military as an intelligence and surveillance officer. Because of the time he spent in the military, his training gave him a good understanding about the technology available to spy on someone.

"That's great, Mike, but what does that have to do with me and the trouble I seem to be in?" Nathan queried.

"Well, Nathan, during the time you were away that I spent watching Jasper at your cabin, I found your cabin was bugged," Mike revealed.

"BUGGED?" Nathan blurted out.

Mike proceeded to show Nathan where every device had been planted in his cabin. Nathan knew immediately that it was Keith Weathers, and that David Greene must have been the installer.

"Mike," Nathan whispered, "If they're listening in now, then they know we're on to them."

"No worries, Nathan," Mike chuckled. "Part of my expertise in the military was dismantling the spying devices I had planted.

"I'm fairly sure this David Greene is spending some long hours trying to figure out why he's lost the signal, thanks to yours truly. This guy knows his stuff, but he's never run into the likes of me," Mike jokingly quipped.

"Just in case, so that you know, the equipment is right across your property line on the McKenzie's land," Mike revealed like a pirate telling where he had buried the treasure. "It's buried in a grey tote underneath a cross I made from pine branches," Mike added.

"Mike, you sure are a man of many surprises," Nathan replied with a laugh. "I'm sure glad you're on my side!"

Nathan knew that if he didn't settle this with Keith Weathers, that Keith would discover a way to prove that Nathan Peerless ran every scam and crime ring in America.

Robin had tried to call a few times since Nathan arrived back at home, but he decided it was best not to speak with her. She had chosen her side, and he needed to put her behind him.

He sat out on his porch with his dog and enjoyed the crisp air that he relished so much. Pastor Mike was rolling up the gravel road that led to his cabin. Nathan recognized the beat-up old Jeep that Mike loved so much. He was glad that Mike was coming to visit. His company meant so much to him, and Mike passed no judgement upon Nathan for his struggles with his faith and relationship with God.

It had been a while since Nathan had communed with God. He, like so many Christians, felt like he had let God down and God had left him. For the first time in his life, he felt like he was not worthy to receive God's love, or gifts.

Mike sat with Nathan on the porch and stroked the neck of Jasper who was always receptive to good petting.

"It's been a while since you've been to Church, hasn't it, Nate?" Mike innocently asked.

"I know what you're trying to do here, Mike," Nathan responded.

Light conversation continued on the cabin porch, and sometime later, Mike stood up to head back down to his church. As their afternoon visit drew to a close, Mike offered a parting invitation to Nathan.

"Hey, I sent postcards out in the mail to all the locals. We're having a special service next Sunday to pray for physical and spiritual healing in the community.

"No pressure, Nathan. You've done your duty; I'll take it from here. I just want my friend to be there and to come over to the house for dinner after Church."

Nathan knew that Mike meant he was going to grill some of his elk steaks. It was almost impossible to refuse those steaks!

"I'll think about it, Mike," Nathan replied. "Can I bring Jasper?"

"You can come *only* if you bring Jasper," Mike replied as he started his Jeep, stuck his hand out the window and waved.

CHAPTER 29
MOTHER & DAUGHTER

Despite not ever sleeping very well, Angie knew she had to get up. Even if she could stay in bed longer, her mind would not let her escape thinking about what the voice she heard in the Church parking lot meant. It was strange enough that the same voice had called out the name of Nathan, but this latest encounter was a mystery.

She sat up and, swinging her legs from the bed, placed her feet in her slippers. She forced herself upright and proceeded into the bathroom. Her walk was more of a shuffle today as she moved down the hallway towards Sandy's bedroom. Angie stood in the doorway of her crippled daughter's room and saw she was awake.

"Good morning, sweetie," Angie said.

"Hi, mom," Sandy replied.

"Do you want some help getting up today, honey, or would you rather mom leave you to do it yourself?" Angie asked.

"Mommy," Sandy reluctantly spoke, "I know I'm supposed to try and get up and into my wheelchair myself, but, but...."

"What is it, sweetheart?" Angie inquired.

Tears began to flow from Sandy's eyes and down her cheeks like a steadily trickling mountain brook. "It hurts too bad to do it anymore," Sandy cried. "I need help!"

Angie felt the tears well up in her own eyes from hearing the cry for help coming from her daughter. She wanted to help, and to feel needed in Sandy's life, but not like this. Not at this expense. She fought back the tears and moved to Sandy's bedside. Tucking her right arm under Sandy's back, and grasping onto her right arm, Angie pulled her daughter to a sitting position.

"You've been doing such a good job without me, Sandra," Angie offered up in a praising manner. "Today is just to show you that you are getting better, but you still need your mom!"

Angie said it, but in her heart she believed her daughter was getting worse. The fits of pain were more frequent, and she was afraid Sandy would overdose from the pain pills just trying to exist. After assisting Sandy into her wheelchair and pushing her into the kitchen, she decided this was as good of time as any to tell Sandy what she had decided.

"Sandy, I've been thinking," Angie offered in a pondering fashion, "Maybe getting out of this house for a bit would do us both some good. Maybe we should go to that service at Evergreen Evangelical on Sunday. I don't buy in to most of what they say or do there, but the folks that go to that church are good people."

Sandy, who sat slightly slouched down in her chair, replied, "Well, it can't hurt me anymore than I already am, can it?"

Angie wasn't positive, but since offering to go to the church services, Sandy seemed to perk up for the rest of the day. Later in the week Sandy had a follow-up visit with Dr. Johnson to check on her progress. It would be good for Angie to get an update on Sandy's status and ask if the doctor could help her with the pain management. One thing she knew for sure is that Dr. Johnson and his wife attended Evergreen Evangelical. Angie would make sure she got his opinion on the upcoming services. She also would ask if they would be attending the services. "A good mix of medicine and religion might be the right stuff to help Sandy," Angie considered.

Sandy had always been an active child, smart, too. Everybody would comment that she was the spitting image of Angie and, with jet black hair that she wore in a ponytail just like her mother, she and Angie believed it. Growing up, she hadn't been very interested in sports, despite having the physique of an athlete, everything she liked were *girl* things.

Angie never spoke of the absence of her father and Sandy never seemed to be interested. Mom and daughter were two peas in a pod and Sandy worshipped her mom. Both knew very little of the world outside their mountain town of Evergreen. Sure, they ventured into Denver occasionally, but travel to vacation lands or outside of Colorado wasn't really something Angie was interested in or needed. Sandy, who always followed her mother, was equally a home body and vacations were usually spent at home, renting movies and taking walks or cooking yummy desserts.

Still, Sandy often wondered privately what it would be like to have a dad. At school she would watch other kids get picked up by their fathers and she would imagine what they did at home. Did their dad watch movies with them? Read books? Exactly what did dads do? She never felt deprived because her mom was everything she needed.

When the day came that Sandy asked what happened to her grandparents, her mother answered her as honestly as possible.

"When I got pregnant with you baby, my mother and father asked me to leave. They didn't approve of anybody having a baby outside of being married and I had nowhere to go," she continued.

Her mother went on to tell her that despite her mother and father not wanting to know her or to love her, Grandma Bessie and Grandpa Jed did. Jedidiah and Elizabeth Black, Angie's grandparents, lived in Evergreen, Colorado, and Angie came to them, pregnant and in need of a home. Sandy's grandparents, Angie's mother and father never knew Sandy had been born in Evergreen and that these mountains would always be part of her.

Once she asked her mother if she had known her grandparents because Sandy never had. Angie and Sandy lived in the house that her mom's grandfather built. Sandy fell in love with the stories that her mother told her about Grandpa Jed because they are so foreign to the life Sandy lives. Angie's Grandma was a short, stocky woman who loved to cook and bake. Angie often wondered why she wasn't four hundred pounds, having spent quite a bit of time with Grandma Bessie. They homesteaded the property and Jed worked long hours running a lumber mill.

Sandy wished she had known them, especially Grandpa Jed.

CHAPTER 30
PLACE HOLDER

Twisting the knob that would allow David to scan different frequencies, he slammed his fist down on his desk with frustration that he was unable to hear any activity or noise coming through his spying devices. He grabbed his headphones and tossed them across the room. Losing contact with someone he was conducting surveillance on had never happened to him before. "Sure, I have to make adjustments every now and then, but I've never lost contact totally," he moaned.

It was bad enough that he was experiencing technical difficulties that he wasn't sure how he could remedy short of walking up to Nathan's cabin and confront him with, "Hey, Healer Boy, I've planted listening devices all over your cabin and I need to go inside to find out why they aren't working," he kidded himself to try and relieve his anxiety.

What was worse was he was going to have to tell Keith.

Glancing at his cell phone he decided that he must pivot, and pivot immediately. Scanning the contact list on his phone, David selected the number to some associates he had used before, when boots-on-the-ground were required. Selecting the number, a short time later, David had commissioned this contact to arrive in Evergreen, Colorado, and to get eyes and ears on Nathan Peerless.

He reluctantly selected Keith's number and waited impatiently for him to answer. After a few rings, Keith's voice answered. "What's up, David? Important news, I assume, since you've interrupted me with this call."

"Sorry, Keith. I didn't want to disturb you, but I thought you needed to know that I've lost surveillance contact with Peerless."

There was a long pause before Keith responded to the news he had just been provided with. "Can it be corrected?" Keith inquired.

"I doubt it. I've tried everything to regain contact," David admitted, knowing this revelation wouldn't be very well received.

"Well then, we can assume it's one of two issues. Either you aren't as competent as I was led to believe, or you've been discovered. I suspect it's the latter."

David couldn't answer.

"What's your plan, Mr. Greene?" Keith asked, using David's last name, which meant that he was deeply disappointed or, perhaps, even angry.

"I've sent some reliable associates to Evergreen. They will be inconspicuous and deliver information on every move Peerless makes."

"I want… let me correct myself… I *need* constant reports on his activity. I have a great deal riding on him messing up," Keith revealed.

"Messing up?" David quizzed.

"Mr. Peerless has settled our little contract dispute. Let's just say that it cost him a great deal of money to remedy what he did to poor little me. He has also agreed to disband his ministry and cease and desist from conducting any healing events in lieu of the Tennessee Attorney General pressing to get any felony charges against him."

"Why the tracking then?" David couldn't help but push to get an answer.

"Let's just say I have *personal* business with Nathan Peerless," Keith said.

"Copy that, boss," David acknowledged.

"I need to know if this man so much as farts. I have a lot riding on this, Mr. Greene."

As he ended the call, David cringed at the thought that, despite the stakes being raised in this saga between Keith Weathers and Nathan Peerless, he was responsible for dealing the cards.

CHAPTER 31
RESULTS

She leaned back in her high back leather chair and gazed out her office window. Robin was one half in the moment and the other half yearning for a lost love. She set down the contract she had been reviewing which contained the agreement between a replacement evangelist and Nashville Entertainment.

Her cell phone rang and, looking at the caller ID, she could see it was Keith. Picking up the phone, she said her usual greetings.

"Howdy, my prized assistant. You done going over the contract yet?" Keith inquired, knowing that he needn't worry about her efficiencies.

"I'm done with it. All looks good and I was about ready to have it sent certified mail to our newest client to sign," Robin acknowledged.

"Excellent! I believe he will be well received by the public, not to mention he's charming and charismatic," Keith added.

"Yes, he sure is. Young, but charismatic," Robin agreed.

"Do I detect that you are a little smitten by our replacement?" Keith said in a clearly joking matter.

"I think one evangelist/healer in my lifetime is probably enough. Been there, done that," Robin replied simultaneously with Keith chuckling on the other end of the call. "I thought you weren't available this morning. You said you were out of the office at a Dr. appointment until this afternoon," she casually inquired since his call had surprised her.

"I am. Waiting for the doctor to come in. Thought I'd give you a quick call to make sure everything was under control. As anticipated, you're doing a great job," Keith responded.

"Good luck. See you soon," Robin said as she ended the call. Keith's praise helped to relieve the anxiety she was feeling. Her confidence that everything wasn't crashing down around her was subtly fading. Still, a minute didn't go by that she didn't think about Nathan and what he was doing.

As soon as she ended the call with Keith, her phone rang again, indicating that David Greene was on the line. Surprised to hear her voice, David responded when she answered the call. "Uh, hello, Robin. I didn't expect to have you answer. I was trying to call Keith."

"Good to hear your voice also," Robin sarcastically replied. "Keith's at an appointment and won't be available until this afternoon. He's forwarded his calls to me. Is there something I can do for you?"

David was perturbed at her response. This was all so new and strange to him. He thought he would never see the day where Keith left a woman in charge. "Nope, but can you leave Keith a message that I called? Nothing urgent, just wanted to provide him with an update on a project we're working on."

Robin could detect that David was hiding something. His mannerism and voice gave him away. Plus, Keith had never mentioned any project that he was working on exclusively with David. Keith had been entrusting almost everything to her lately.

"Suit yourself. I'll give Keith your message," she replied as she hung up.

David sat at his computer reviewing the image that his associates had sent him. He scanned the image of a postcard that they had happened upon once they arrived in Evergreen. Staring at the text and graphics of the postcard, front and back, over and over, he had the feeling that this was the answer that Keith was looking for. This was the answer that was going to deliver him, once again, back to the good graces of his boss.

He loathed doctors. It was their arrogance about punctuality that he believed made him the angriest. Keith had been sitting in the examination room dressed in only his underwear and a light blue hospital gown, waiting for the doctor, for almost forty-five minutes. If he had to read the poster on the wall detailing the circulatory system anymore, he thought he might just get dressed and leave. He knew he couldn't.

The clinical trials that he was forced to begin because Nathan Peerless had failed to deliver him from his disease, was, as of right now, his only hope, and he needed to find out what, if any, progress the experimental regimen had yielded for him.

Finally, with a soft tap on the examination room door, Dr. Benjamin Sing entered. "Hello, Keith," Sing greeted an already impatient patient.

"Hello, doctor. Do you have some news for me? Good or bad, I need some answers."

Not a physician to beat around the bush, Dr. Sing was equally glad to forget the pleasantries and get on with the consultation. "Keith, the tests are showing some good progress. Your blood work is, surprisingly, showing improvement and we see some reduction of masses in your lungs."

Keith smiled a broad smile as he tilted his head towards the ceiling with closed eyes.

"So, with that said, how have you been feeling?" the doctor asked, as he began to place his stethoscope on Keith's upper back.

Keith felt no reason to hide anything and answered honestly. "I have good days, and I have bad days. Since I began the treatments, I must admit, the good days have been more frequent."

"Very good. Well, we are making positive progress, but we have a long way to go," Dr. Sing proclaimed.

As Keith departed the Clinic, once his review with Dr. Sing was over, he felt elated. Climbing into the back seat of the SUV, he gave a pleasant greeting to his driver. Any sign of kindness or even being cordial from Keith was almost non-existent as of late. The driver found Keith's demeanor today refreshing.

After settling into his seat, Keith couldn't help but mumble to himself. "Well, well, Mr. Peerless. Perhaps I had placed too much faith in your God and religion, and you, instead of trusting science." As the SUV pulled out into the roadway to begin its journey back to Nashville Amusements' corporate office, Keith's phone rang, and he gleefully answered the call.

"My oh my, must have good news based on your attitude," Robin expounded.

"Nope, but I got a sucker," Keith laughed uncontrollably until a coughing fit overtook his glee. Once it had subsided and Keith swallowed some water he commented, "Yes, you can tell it was a good visit. I'll share more with you when we're face to face. In the meantime, to what do I owe the pleasure of hearing your delightful voice?" Keith cooed uncharacteristically.

"David Greene called looking for you. He said it wasn't urgent; he just had some news about a project you two were working on. I suspect it might be a little more urgent than he indicated."

Keith was intrigued by what she had just said. "Okay, I'll call him when I get a chance. He's correct, the project we're working on is nothing important. Don't fret. If it were important, you would definitely be involved."

The call ended with Keith assuring her that he would see her soon at the office. He couldn't wait to call David. He hoped it was good news about their wayward client. Although the results of the experimental trial were positive, Keith wasn't prepared to lose his ace-in-the hole that he might have to pull and reveal his hand.

CHAPTER 32
FADING HOPE

David clicked the send icon on the email and attachment associated with it, sending it to Keith. He had already instructed his associates that they needed to be at that service on Sunday at Evergreen Evangelical. He *must* have a full report of every move the *target* made. He borrowed the words of his superior, "I need to know if he so much as farts!"

David was pleased with the response he received from Keith. The statement from his boss that "This could be exactly what I've been waiting for," brought great satisfaction to him and gave him hope that Robin would be excluded from any future endeavors between him and Keith. He really didn't know what Keith meant by his statement 'this could be exactly what I've been waiting for' but it wasn't his job to understand everything Keith said or did.

Sitting in the chair next to a small laptop computer that Dr. Johnson used to record notes on his patient's charts, Angie Black looked at her daughter with a perturbed face. "I'm glad we don't have to be anywhere else today, huh, honey?" Angie said.

"I could have easily passed away by now, and you too," Sandy replied with a smirk.

A short time later, Dr. Johnson tapped on the door to the exam room that contained the girls and entered. He was a pleasant man with a good bedside manner who always wore hospital scrubs with a white exam coat over them. A slightly balding man, he stood at about six feet and was of average build. Angie believed he was the best doctor they could have hoped for in this mountain town. He was always very caring about Sandy's welfare, so because of that, Angie appreciated Dr. Johnson.

"Hello, Angela and Sandra," Dr. Johnson said as he entered the room. He never called them by their shortened names and Sandy always delighted in that.

Both girls gave their greetings back to Dr. Johnson. The doctor proceeded to bring the girls up to date on Sandy's exam, lab work, and MRI.

His news wasn't good.

The MRI showed that Sandy's spine was continuing to degenerate and physical therapy was not appearing to help. He felt that Sandy most likely faced eventual permanent paralysis.

"What about the pain though?" Sandy inquired.

"Well, the pain is actually good news," Dr. Johnson replied with raised eyebrows. "As long as you still feel pain, the nerves are still firing," he continued.

He went on to explain that the pain would become less and less as the degeneration continued. "I don't want you to have to suffer until the nerve endings begin to die. I'll put you on a more aggressive pain management program which can help," he offered.

Dr. Johnson went on to explain that the more aggressive pain management treatment would require her to be on an IV drip which would inhibit her movement. In fact, she would have to stay in bed for longer periods of time. Sandy couldn't decide what was worse. The pain, or being constantly attached to an IV.

"Will you let me talk to your mom alone, Sandra?" He asked.

Sandy excused herself from the exam room and rolled her wheelchair out into the waiting area to allow her mom and Dr. Johnson to discuss her dismal fate. Once she was gone, Dr. Johnson looked at Angie with a defeated look.

"Angela, I have honestly done all I can do for Sandra, except for the pain management," he admitted. "I can refer you to a specialist in Denver to give you another opinion, but I just can't give you a positive outcome based on where we're at now," Dr. Johnson added.

Angie Black felt the most despair she had felt in several years. Nothing seemed real. Tears began to well up in her eyes and she thanked the doctor for everything he had done. As she began to get up to leave the exam room, Angie remembered to ask Dr. Johnson about his faith. "Doctor," Angie spoke softly, "I understand you are a man of faith, well, at least you go to Church. Do you believe there is any truth that God heals people?" she asked in a tearful voice expecting a man of science to not have that belief.

The doctor grabbed Angie's hands and looked her straight in her eyes. It shocked Angie that he was this forward. "Angela, I'm a scientist. A man of medicine. I also believe Jesus Christ is God, and is far greater than I." Angie felt the truth in his words.

"Because of this, I believe that God gave me science and medicine to use as a *gift*. Believing that medicine and faith can heal your body, but more important than your body, they can heal your soul. This is something I steadfastly endorse."

Angie shook her head up and down wanting to believe what the doctor was saying. She told him that she would see him at the revival services at Evergreen Evangelical on Sunday, because Sandy had asked her to go.

Dr. Johnson let go of Angie's hands and opened the door for her to leave.

"Good, we welcome you *both* on Sunday. Yet, as important as it is that Sandra has asked you to go, you need to consider yourself. God loves you, Angela," Dr. Johnson replied with a smile.

"If I can suggest something to you before you leave, I would try and delay the new pain management therapy for a couple of days. It will make Sandra very incoherent for a while, and I feel that she needs to be awake and alert to hear Mike's message on Sunday."

Angie tried to wipe the tears from her eyes before meeting her daughter in the waiting room. She was sure Sandy could tell she had been crying.

CHAPTER 33
SHOPPING TRIP

He rolled over in bed to be greeted by a large black paw reaching out to cover his forearm. With one eye only slightly open, Nathan called out to Jasper, "Hey, how did you get up here?"

Nathan knew that Jasper was not about to reveal his secret of how he got up on the bed, so he felt compelled to just greet his new bed partner with a healthy ear scratch.

"Well, Jasper, my boy, what's on the calendar for today?" Nathan inquired, knowing full well Saturday would be up to him.

He went onto explain to his cabin mate that he guessed he needed to go to church tomorrow since he was also invited over to Pastor Mike's for dinner. "Better buy a much-needed new pair of blue jeans, or the congregation might think I was a homeless man."

Nathan decided he would go to the Mercantile, then to the feed store to buy Jasper's dog food. "And even though you finagled your way up onto the bed last night and aren't a very good boy, maybe, just maybe, I'll buy you a new collar," he called out to Jasper in a playful voice.

He decided it had to be a Denver Bronco dog collar. Nathan was a Colorado boy, and the Broncos were his team. Naturally, they had to be Jasper's team too.

The leaves shimmered on the spring aspen tree branches. The morning air was still crisp and cool. Perfect weather in Nathan's world. Striding out to his old pick-up, he noticed it needed a good cleaning, so he would also get that chore done while he was out.

Button fly Levi's were the only pair of jeans for him. As he exited the dressing room to make sure he could still fit into a thirty-four-inch waist with a thirty-six-inch inseam, Nathan noticed a few pairs of women's black UGH boots on display. He couldn't help but wonder what Robin was doing today. Nathan still missed her. Her touch, her beauty, her eyes!

Nathan pulled himself out of the sulking mood he was in from those rehashed memories of Robin and returned the jeans back to the table from where they had come. The desire to buy new clothes diminished after seeing those boots on display. He thanked the Mercantile store owner for his help and left the store without buying anything. He thought to himself that if the congregation at Evergreen Evangelical didn't like his old *ratty* clothes, then too bad!

Jasper fared much better in the purchase area as Nathan drove home with a fancy new Denver Bronco dog collar, rawhide treats and a huge bag of food. Nathan saw the do-it-yourself carwash on Main Street, so he pulled his pickup into the open stall. After spending an hour washing the truck and vacuuming the interior, Nathan wasn't too sure that the truck looked any better than before!

"Oh well, what should anybody expect from a broken-down faith healer with holy jeans," Nathan thought to himself with all the sense of humor he could muster now. Out of the corner of his eye Nathan spotted the Burger Barn. It had been almost two years sense he had partaken in this culinary delight due to Robin not eating fast food. Nathan drove past the entrance and thought he should probably go home and fix some vegetable pasta and a salad instead of indulging in the caloric feast presented by the Burger Barn. A short moment later Nathan pulled a very illegal U-turn on Main Street and entered the drive-thru of the Burger Barn.

As he drove down the street towards his cabin, a mixture of catsup, mustard and mayo dripped onto his holy jeans as he sank his teeth into a double stacked burger. His delight and pleasure from inhaling this burger felt so good. He couldn't help but wonder what Robin would say if she saw him eating this treat!

He presumed she would probably say, "good thing you didn't buy those jeans today because they will be too tight if you keep eating like that," Nate chuckled to himself.

He pulled up to his cabin and climbed out of the cab of his truck. Jasper began to whine at the sight of his master returning home. Nathan walked to the door of the cabin and let Jasper come out onto the porch. Sitting down in his favorite porch chair, Nathan looked into the greasy paper bag provided by the Burger Barn.

"Well, Jasper, your ex-mommy wouldn't be too happy with me today," Nathan confessed.

Nathan reached into the paper bag and extracted another double stack burger. He laughed as he unwrapped it and proceeded to eat the second burger.

"Oh look, Jasper," Nathan laughed as he scanned the bottom of the bag. "Amazingly enough, there's a burger in here for you too!"

Several states away Robin Gunderson opened the top of a plastic container that carried the mixed-greens salad she had bought at the local delicatessen. As she opened the Italian dressing that accompanied the salad to pour over the top, she stopped.

Nathan was ever present on her mind and today it wasn't in a good way. She couldn't help but shake the feeling that something was going to happen that would change everything. Sticking her fork into her salad she brought the lettuce to her mouth but once again stopped before inserting it. She sniffed the contents of the salad that were on her fork. Everything smelled and seemed normal but, for some reason that she couldn't identify, she smelled the aroma of a fast-food hamburger in the surrounding air.

CHAPTER 34
RESTORATION

The morning sky was slightly overcast as Nathan finished shaving and began his preparation to get ready for church. He felt nervous and was very uncomfortable. He didn't usually feel nervous about going to church, but he guessed it was because he felt embarrassed. Had God let him down, or even worse, had he let God down?

Nathan had lately considered that perhaps God had taken away his gift because *he* had allowed others to manipulate him instead of obeying God, and thus wasn't mature enough to use God's power.

Either way, he hoped this was his opportunity to communicate with God once again even though it might not be with a divine understanding. Nathan missed the Lord, and he needed to worship him again. So many aspects of Nathan's future hinged on his faith and how he managed it.

Money had been provided for him to be an evangelist and missionary. He had been the benefactor of a lot of money that people gave to him because they were grateful. He thought to himself, "sure, that money was from people that felt like he was instrumental in healing them," but to just walk away from practicing his faith and witness because he was discouraged would be a sin.

God had to show him the way to honor those people that believed in him and believed in his God. He needed to grow up and get back to sharing his faith with others. He just felt nervous that the results of his recent past might prohibit people from accepting, or worse, listening to him. If Nathan could no longer heal anybody, what did he really have to offer?

"Baby steps," Nathan whispered to himself. He realized going to services today was a start to those steps, but he couldn't just put himself out there. He just didn't possess that confidence. Instead, he would just blend into the background. He really wasn't prepared to tell anybody what had happened, how he was labeled a fraud, but more importantly, what happened to his lovely fiancé.

Taking one last look in the mirror, he realized he looked and felt older than he had ever witnessed before. Jasper thought he looked just fine because his tail thumped on the bedroom floor as he watched his master ready himself.

"I'll swing by after church, boy, to pick you up, and you can go to Mike's house with me." Nathan spoke to Jasper as if he were a baby. He grabbed the tattered New American Standard bible that he had carried for years. This was the bible his mother had given to him when he was a boy. The leather cover was worn in spots, but Nathan never considered getting a new bible. He chuckled that the bible was like his blue jeans; old, worn, and broken in. It had belonged to his Granddad. Nathan had no recollection of his grandfather, or even of his father. His mother had told him stories of the men that had preceded him in history, but it was his mother and grandmother that raised him and recognized his gift.

Angie sat brushing Sandy's hair with extra care so as not to pull on it and cause her daughter any discomfort. She was delighted in Sandy's attitude today. She showed no signs of irritation about having to get ready to go to church.

"I'm excited, mommy," Sandy chirped.

"Yes, me too. I'm not sure why," Angie chimed in.

Sandy pondered her mother's remark and decided to respond to it. "I think I know why we're excited."

"Oh, do you now, young lady? And just what might be our reason?"

Sandy rolled her wheelchair to a window that faced the front of the property. Stopping the chair, she gazed out the window at the marvelous morning that was forming in the Colorado mountains and offered her perspective, "We're excited because we're going to meet Jesus there."

Angie had no comeback to refute her daughter's wisdom and checked her makeup one more time before grabbing the car keys and ushering Sandy out the front door.

Nathan drove his truck into Evergreen Evangelical's parking lot. He parked near the back of the parking lot to not attract any attention and smiled because it looked like the turnout today was going to be very good. He looked up to the sky and spoke to God.

"Lord, may today be a good day for people to come to know you. Thanks for bringing me back to see you!" Nathan grabbed his worn bible and climbed out of his truck. He couldn't help but notice two sparrows that were bouncing from tree limb to tree limb, singing and chirping to each other. He started a slow stroll to the front of the church planning on staying as incognito as possible. It didn't work.

It seemed like the entire town was aware that he was coming to the services. He was a bit overwhelmed with the kindness that was being bestowed upon him as many of the congregation made it a point to come up to him and show their appreciation that he was there. Nathan was relieved by the response he encountered and couldn't help but be relieved by the genuine fellowship and comfort provided by the folks of Evergreen, but he was committed to hanging out near the back of the church and sharing worship in the quietest way possible.

"That's our target," one of the strangers whispered to his partner as Nathan strolled by them, accompanied by his entourage.

Pastor Mike would have none of the stealth posture his friend was taking. He spotted Nathan holding a cup of coffee and standing near the back of the sanctuary. He ran up to Nathan, extending his hand in exuberance.

"Great to see you, brother," Mike offered as if he were a long-lost friend.

"Well, I assumed that the steaks would be off the table if I didn't come. Jasper has been excited all week and I didn't want to disappoint him," Nathan chuckled.

Mike responded, "Not at all, I like Jasper way too much to ruin his day because his master couldn't come to church!"

Both men embraced each other in general joy and pleasure that they were brothers in Christ.

Just when Nathan thought he might get to return to being obscure in the back row, Mike pointed at an open seat towards the middle of the sanctuary and asked, "Nathan, can you do me a big favor?"

"Sure, Mike, what do you need me to do?"

"I have some important folks that are sitting there in the wheelchair row, and it would be a big help to me if you could go sit with them. They both used to attend services here, and now they've returned after being absent for a long time."

"Kinda like me, huh?" Nathan acknowledged.

"Let's just say this is the first service of this nature they've ever attended, and I just want somebody there that can answer their questions."

Nathan could barely see over the crowd that was pouring in and looked towards where the visitors would be sitting. He made out that one of them was a young girl sitting in the aisle and she was in a wheelchair.

Mike proclaimed, "Hey, come with me and I'll introduce you to them. They're a local family here in Evergreen. Angie Black and her daughter, Sandy." Mike motioned for Nathan to follow him. "I'm sure they'll have some questions, and I can't think of anybody better to answer them than you,"

The two strangers waited patiently for Nathan to take his seat. All the while, one of the men had a recording device and made sure to capture every move that Nathan made. He became slightly irritated when the pastor of the church directed their target to follow him to the front of the church. That area was already filled except for one seat next to a woman accompanying a young girl in a wheelchair. He eagerly glanced around the church for somewhere to gain a clear vantage to videotape their reason for being there.

Nathan followed Mike forward to where Angie and Sandy had been greeting other congregation members. He introduced Nathan to Sandy first, then waited a few seconds for Angie to turn from a conversation she was having with another couple. Angie turned to greet Pastor Mike.

"Angie, I would like you to meet a very good friend of mine, and a fellow Pastor, Nathan Peerless."

Angie was speechless and stupefied, for standing before her was a tall, good-looking man with a smile that could melt her soul. She was certain the red in her face eclipsed the rouge she had applied that morning. She also couldn't shake the fact that this man she had just been introduced to bore the same name that she had heard whispered to her in the dead of night.

The recent events of his relationship with Robin had soured Nathan on the possibility that he would ever become romantically involved with another woman. He had let himself fall head over heels for a woman that deceived him in every way possible. Now, standing before him was a woman he had just met, along with her daughter, no less, and he found himself attracted to her.

This woman was everything Robin was not. Complete opposites. Angie Black was petite, with jet black hair tied into a ponytail which showed no pretense of being overly sophisticated. She was naturally a pretty woman. Nathan could tell she didn't wear much makeup, and he was convinced she didn't need to.

"Pleasure to meet you, Mrs. Black" Nathan said.

Angie replied in a somewhat bashful way, "Oh, it's not Mrs., and you can call me Angie."

Nathan was secretly glad to hear there wasn't a Mr. Black in the picture, although he reprimanded himself for even having those thoughts. To move the conversation away from his fumbling introduction to Angie, Nathan turned his attention towards her daughter. Nathan knelt on bended knee in order to not tower over Sandy and possibly intimidate her.

"I'm glad you're joining us today, Sandy" Nathan spoke in a gentle and caring way.

"Say, would you be okay if I sat next to you during the service today?" Nathan asked.

Sandy replied with a big smile on her face "Sure, Nathan, and since my mom is standing behind you nodding her head up and down, I guess she approves!"

Nathan turned to see an embarrassed Angie smiling at him with that look of *I'm going to kill you* directed towards Sandy.

Hoping to cut the tension and awkwardness, Nathan replied in his best Texas accent, "Hey, sometimes Pastor Mike can be so darn confusing with his messages that I feel it is my duty to help y'all out."

All three laughed and as the music began to play in the sanctuary, Sandy, in her wheelchair, Nathan and Angie sitting next to each other, settled in as the services began.

As the church band played uplifting songs, and the choir sang the lyrics of inspiration, the congregation stood, clapped their hands, and raised them to the Lord. Angie couldn't help but glance over at Sandy who did her best to participate despite being confined to a wheelchair. It probably wasn't the right time for Angie to pray. In fact, she didn't really know *how* to pray, but seeing Sandy sitting there, a young woman, crippled, who should have been standing and singing like the rest of the congregation, she pleaded for God to heal her daughter.

Angie prayed to the God of the bible that she would do anything to have her daughter be physically whole again. She felt the tears well up in her eyes like they had done so often lately. Angie raised her hands to the Lord and began to sing the songs of praise and worship. Nathan smiled at Angie. He wasn't sure she was a believer when he met her, but something was happening at this very moment. He hoped he could visit with her and Sandy to learn more about their lives. He was particularly interested in Sandy's story. Was she crippled from birth or what might have brought her to this life in a wheelchair?

Pastor Mike's sermons were always the best he had ever heard, Nathan thought to himself. He had never considered himself as talented in preaching the gospel as his friend. In fact, he always joked that every time he heard Mike preach, he got saved again! Today was no different as Mike was laying down every reason to believe that Jesus was Lord and Savior.

Looking over at Sandy, Nathan felt her hand on his forearm. She reached over to Nathan and leaned into him to ask her question.

"Nathan, can God heal me today if I believe?" Sandy asked with a small tear forming in her right eye.

Nathan replied in the loudest whisper he could, "Jesus can do anything. In fact, he does do everything!"

Sandy acknowledged what Nathan had just said and continued to listen to Pastor Mike. As Mike closed the message to the multitude in the sanctuary, he offered the salvation prayer as invitation to any, and all, that believed they had met the living God today. Sandy and Angie listened intently to Mike's words and bowed their heads as Mike prayed the salvation prayer.

At the close of his prayer, Mike offered his usual ritual of inviting all who had prayed the salvation prayer, and now truly believed, to come forward to the stage and the staff would be available to answer any questions, or pray additional prayers with them. Most importantly, new believers could find out *What Now?*

Nathan said his Amen and was elated to see Sandy begin her journey up to the front. She was focused on nobody, she showed no interest in how people might view her as a cripple, she began her roll forward in her wheelchair to truly begin her journey as a believer. Angie excused herself as she stepped in front of Nathan to hurry up and follow her daughter. He felt blessed to be in the presence of these two new souls for Christ.

Nathan wasn't on the staff of Evergreen Evangelical but felt compelled to follow Sandy and Angie to the front. It looked like Mike was going to need some help today. Nathan glanced up at Mike who acknowledged his presence at the front of the altar and mouthed the words *"thank you."*

Nathan came up from behind Sandy and Angie and leaned down so the girls could both hear him.

"Sandy and Angie, have you both accepted Jesus Christ as your personal savior today?" Nathan inquired.

Both girls had tears of joy in their eyes and Sandy replied "Oh, Nathan, I came today for such selfish reasons. I came looking for God to heal me. I had no idea how much he suffered for me!"

Angie listened closely to what her daughter had just said to Nathan. "Can you show us how to live for Christ?" Angie earnestly asked.

Nathan stared deep into Angie's eyes and then looked at Sandy and said "Ladies, it would be an answer to *my* prayer to do just that!" He got down on his knees and instructed Angie to do the same. They formed a circle and held each other by the hand. Once they had grasped each other's hand,

Nathan bowed his head and asked Angie and Sandy to join him in prayer.

The two strangers had moved closer to the altar to ensure that all the video of Nathan would be clear and concise. Neither man was sure what significance the action they were seeing might have to impact anything, but their job wasn't to question the motivation.

This is the moment that those who attended this service and had ventured to the altar at Evergreen Evangelical would talk about for years.

Nathan lost all sense of the world around him. All he could see was white, almost pure as snow surrounding him until it totally engulfed him. No longer could he sense the feel of Angie or Sandy's hands in his. He felt a coolness in his hands like a long-lost friend. He likened it to when you roll a snowball with your bare hands, freezing cold, and this sensation had been long absent from him.

Then it happened! The voice of his God spoke to Nathan. The voice of God brought into view for Nathan an image, eclipsing the white, like a movie being projected onto a white screen, the figure of a young woman. Standing, but transparent. The image that was projected seemed to glow. Through the transparency Nathan noticed an illuminated spinal cord. The illumination showed damage beyond the abilities of any man to repair.

He wondered if this could be Sandy, but what confused him the most was the figure was standing with their arms outstretched to Heaven. He looked at the complexity of the human spine, attached to the human brain, acting as the conduit and source for all feelings and impulses. Then, his hands began too gradually warm. After what seemed like only just a few moments, Nathan's hands began to glow just like the image he saw before him. There was no pain or discomfort associated with the heat sensation whatsoever, but it was different than any he had ever felt before.

Those that were not caught in the trance of what was occurring before them saw flashing lights of color descending from the peak of the ceiling. The colors yellow, red, orange and blue formed a vacuum around Nathan, Angie and Sandy. Almost like a tornado but without any force of wind or destruction. The funnel was a blanket of peace inside and out.

Nathan raised one arm and extended his index finger, pointing directly at the image, then he touched the standing figure at the top of its spine.

CHAPTER 35
STANDING

Dr. Johnson, along with his wife, Sarah, stood at the church altar in awe. They could not take their eyes off the spectacle they were witnessing. Just to the left of them was Sandy Black, eyes closed, and *standing*! Nathan Peerless was behind her, reaching out with one arm and hand, his index finger slightly touching the top of her neck at the cervical vertebrae.

Nathan's eyes were also closed, as were Angie's, who, standing beside them, was in full prayer. Where Nathan's finger touched Sandy, a glow pulsated from bright to dim. Later, those that witnessed the event would say it looked almost like a firefly had landed on Nate's finger.

Pastor Mike cleared the immediate area around Nathan, Sandy and Angie to avoid anybody bumping into them, or worse, disrupting Nathan. Mike knew exactly what was happening at his altar, but he wasn't sure how it would end. Should Sandy fall, she would almost certainly miss the wheelchair and hurt herself. He just knew, no matter what, he couldn't stop this.

With wide eyes the size of silver dollars, one of the strangers leaned into the other to whisper, "I sure hope you're getting all this."

The doctor had not seen Sandy standing upright for over two years. He was her doctor and knew very well that standing at all was impossible, especially now. Whatever the outcome today, Dr. Johnson was sure he was witnessing a miracle!

Nathan continued to move his finger down the spinal column with the diligence of a skilled surgeon. God continued speaking to him in an audible voice. It was a voice he had longed to hear.

As his touch journeyed down her spine, the transparency would begin to fade, and the true form of the young woman would come into view. As his work was nearing completion, it became very clear to Nathan that this young woman was, indeed, Sandy Black.

With the last area of her spine renewed, Sandy turned towards Nathan. She revealed a glow about her that Nathan had never witnessed before.

"I am healed by the grace of my Lord, Jesus Christ," Sandy called out in triumph.

"Amen, and all praise be to our God," Nathan replied.

In the past, when God used Nathan's touch to heal, Nathan knew when God's work was complete, and he always returned to reality and the amazement of those around him. This time was different. Nathan did not return to reality but turned from Sandy and faced Angie who had no recognition of what had just happened.

His hands were cool but not freezing. The tornado of colors still swirled about them, and he was alone with Angie Black. Angie smiled at Nathan but did not speak. She reached her hands out to Nathan's, and he took them into his. As per usual, Nathan's hands began to warm in anticipation of God's vision and instruction.

This time God did not provide a vision to Nathan of what disease or infliction he would be utilized to heal in Angie. The last couple of years had served the lesson to never again question God as to his purpose, but he couldn't help but be curious about the reason for this meeting with Angie.

Nathan then looked down to discover Angie had let go of one of his hands and extended it towards Nathan's chest. With that hand placed on Nathan's chest she smiled at him.

"Nathan, this healing is for you," God said.

Tears began to flow down his face as he realized that Angie's hand placed on his heart meant that she had been brought to him to heal his broken heart. That very day she had come to know Christ, and now she would be utilized to heal the healer. Nathan had prayed, and God had answered.

The headache she had been nursing was becoming more intense with every waking hour. Robin couldn't help but yearn for the touch of Nathan like she had experienced when she first met him. This time the pain seemed more intense, and she knew that no relief was to come.

Every glorious moment that he felt better had suddenly been thrown out the window. Yesterday was a Saturday for the books. He had gone to his recording studio and felt encouraged to write a song for the first time in a long time. He played his guitar and wrote the music down feeling like he did when he was a younger man. A struggling singer/songwriter once, but now nobody could take advantage of him or his talent. He was Keith Weathers, the man that built the largest entertainment empire in the world.

That was Saturday. A day of triumph. This was Sunday. A day that the pain forbade him from getting out of bed. Too proud to call for help, Keith knew that the faith he had placed in modern medicine might be letting him down. As he lay in a pool of his own urine, he cried.

CHAPTER 36
I WILL KNOW YOU FOR ETERNITY

As the surroundings of Evergreen Evangelical's sanctuary started to come back into view, Nathan could see Angie and others beginning to huddle around him and the girl that had come to the services in a wheelchair but now stood before them.

Angie, with a joyous scream, leaped to where her daughter stood and gave her a hug, although it was a cautious hug. With tears of joy, Sandy embraced her mother like she would never let her go.

"Mommy, see, I'm whole again, praise God!" Sandy barked and looked up towards heaven.

Angie was forced to sit in Sandy's wheelchair as she was overwhelmed and thought she might faint. Dr. Johnson and his wife came over to Sandy and Angie, giving them both a hug.

"God is the great physician and uses us doctors only as tools," Dr. Johnson spoke.

"*Tools*," Angie thought for a moment! She rose to her feet and went over to Nathan who was standing next to Pastor Mike by this time. She embraced Pastor Mike for several minutes and then turned her attention to Nate.

She embraced Nathan like they had been long lost friends. Angie gave Nathan a kiss on his cheek and said, "Bless you, Nathan Peerless. You are truly a tool of God."

Sandy, after being freed from those that wished to have her share her experience of receiving a miracle, came over to where her mother was standing next to Nathan. Sandy reached up and put her arms around Nathan's neck.

"Thank you, Nathan Peerless," she cried softly.

"I know it was God that truly healed me today, but I can't help but feel I will now know you forever!"

Nathan bent down and gave Sandy a little kiss on her cheek and said, "Enjoy this day, sweetheart, and yes, you will now know me for eternity!"

Nathan was overwhelmed with people sharing their experience of witnessing this miracle today and grateful for the kind attention. It was definitely different than he had received lately, and it was reminiscent of the day he healed Paul, but he also couldn't get Angie out of his mind or heart.

He lost track of her a couple of times and was fearful she would get swept away to revel in the miracle and wouldn't get to learn how they might stay in contact with each other.

Did she feel anything about the vision he had?

What exactly did God mean by the healing that *he* received?

Nathan noticed Angie and Sandy speaking with Doctor and Mrs. Johnson. As they were being swept away out of the sanctuary, he saw Angie's head turn to look at him and mouth the words *"don't let them take me!"* He couldn't help but smile as Mike came up to him as the rest of the sanctuary cleared out.

"I honestly don't know how God will ever beat this day, huh Nate?" Mike asked.

"It was a great day for many, Mike! I can honestly say that when he comes to claim his church just might beat this day," Nate replied with a slight chuckle in his voice.

"You're exactly right, Nate, but I think maybe you and God have become friends again," Mike laughed.

After a short period of chit-chat, Nathan turned to walk from the sanctuary to the parking lot. He felt like he could use a short nap to recover before heading over to Mike's place.

"Oh, by the way, I hope you don't mind, I invited Sandy and Angie Black to dinner tonight," Mike revealed.

"There's another miracle," Nathan thought with a big smile on his face.

The strangers pulled into the Best Western Motel parking lot and parked the black SUV in front of their room. Neither man had said anything after leaving Evergreen Evangelical Church. Finally, one of the men had to break the silence. "What the hell was that? What did we just see?"

"I have no idea," the other man replied.

"What do we do now?" the first stranger asked.

"We go inside, pour a long drink, download the video, and call David Greene."

David listened to the tale his associates revealed about their encounter with Nathan Peerless. "So, the girl got up and walked after everything you saw, correct?" He asked the stranger on the phone.

"Yup, exactly as I told you. Every detail," he answered.

After ending the call, David opened the email attachment containing the video of the event. He was excited to send it to Keith. This video could be his ticket to a big reward. After trying several times to open the attachment, every attempt revealed that there was nothing there. The video was blank.

CHAPTER 37
RETRIBUTION

Keith was perturbed and if he wasn't so weak he might have exploded. Despite sensing that his boss wasn't feeling normal, David knew there wasn't any question that he wasn't happy with him.

"You techno nerds. Videos, listening devices, always the newest gadget for you guys," Keith bellowed.

"These associates of mine aren't prone to exaggeration. Both are ex-Navy Seals. I buy into what they witnessed," David forced an option that he hoped Keith would accept.

"Well, I don't care if they were actual seals! Their words do nothing for my plight. I'm going to sleep on this, David, and hope I can find a way for you to redeem your failures of late," Keith expounded as he abruptly ended the call.

David pulled out the glass and poured the whiskey into it. There would be several of these *pours* tonight. He had lost all concern about keeping his senses.

His cell phone rang several times as he waited for whoever was calling to go to voicemail. After leaving a message didn't stop the caller from attempting several more times, Keith picked up his phone to view the caller ID which displayed that it was Robin.

"Robin, so sorry I kept missing your call," Keith said with a sandpaper voice.

"Turn on the local news," Robin prompted, as if demanding he do it.

Fumbling for the remote control that had managed to evade him by being buried in the bed sheets, Keith pointed it at the television on his wall. There was a news reporter standing in front of a church in Evergreen, Colorado, proclaiming that several attendees had witnessed a young, crippled girl, resigned to life in a wheelchair being miraculously healed by a faith healer that had been accused of being a fraud.

"Gotch ya!" Keith profoundly spoke.

"Robin, I want you and David to go immediately and track Nathan down! I'll email you my terms that he must adhere to or face a lot of trouble."

Robin's heart skipped a beat knowing that soon she would see Nathan again.

CHAPTER 38
PEACE AND COMFORT

Later that afternoon Sandy revealed to Nathan that she could feel his touch moving down her spine while God was healing her, but nothing else. Nathan had never had the opportunity to talk to somebody after a healing experience, so this was exhilarating to listen to her describe what it was like, and how it felt. She shared that she didn't feel invaded by Nathan touching her. He never asked her if he could. He just reached out, but as he did, she said it never felt like the touch of a man.

She told everybody attending Mike's elk steak affair that she believed the weirdest moment wasn't when Nathan touched her, but when she heard a voice say, "STAND!"

"I just knew that I must obey, and the Lord would protect me!"

Dr. Johnson was spending time with Angie talking about the next steps in discipleship when the conversation turned towards a medical topic. "Angie, why don't you bring Sandy by my office tomorrow," Dr. Johnson requested. "We can run a few tests. Obviously, quite a lot of things have changed since our last visit," Dr. Johnson proclaimed even though he was selfishly wanting to review God's handywork.

"Obviously," Angie replied with a giggle.

Nathan couldn't help but enjoy the new friendship that had formed between Sandy and Jasper. The dog was reluctant to leave her side except to chase a tennis ball that Sandy would throw for him. He noticed that Sandy wasn't sitting down very much. He guessed she had sat enough for a lifetime, before today.

He didn't want to force himself on Angie and appear too forward, but he also couldn't help but notice she kept looking at him. Finally, Nathan could wait no longer to speak to her. After what seemed like an eternity for these two to begin talking to each other, it soon became an exclusive club that nobody else could join in edgewise.

Angie shared her story with Nathan about never knowing Sandy's father and Nathan shared his story about never being married but being engaged once. She asked a lot of questions about Robin, but Nathan tried to change the course of the conversation every time she was mentioned. He held nothing back in telling Angie that there was no hope of rekindling the relationship between him and Robin and what was gone, was gone.

She seemed to grow more comfortable that Nathan was hopefully *available* because she couldn't help but feel the events of the day meant something. Not just the miracle for her daughter, but the loneliness that she felt. She had no clue the role God had planned for her in all of this, but what had happened at Evergreen Evangelical was real, and she now felt akin to Nathan Peerless

The dinner, as usual, was fantastic and Nathan really did not want the day to end. Angie contained a beauty that Nathan appreciated. Not just because of her appearance, but because she was witty, funny, charming and kind. She was a local mountain girl in every way, and he felt something about her that he never truly felt from Robin. He could only pray she felt the same way about him,

All good things must come to an end and Nathan realized they had overstayed their welcome for the evening. Mike was yawning, and Sandy and Jasper too.

As everybody said their goodbyes and well wishes to each other, Nathan gave Sandy a hug and went over to Angie to let her know just how much he enjoyed her company this evening. Not knowing if he should shake her hand, or give her a friendly side hug in departure, Angie put her arms up to Nathan's shoulders and gave him a light kiss on the lips.

"Any chance you're free tomorrow evening to come over to our house for dinner?" Angie asked, not knowing if she had stepped out of bounds and moved too fast.

"The Avalanche are playing on TV, and I thought I'd make a home-made pot of chili, as Sandy and I love hockey. Oh, and you can bring Jasper. I think Sandy might have found a new boyfriend."

As he drove home, Nathan smiled all the way as he stroked Jasper's head.

Two weeks later Pastor Mike met Nate, Angie, Sandy and Jasper at the Evergreen County Courthouse.

Sandy was the Maid-of-Honor, and Pastor Mike was the Officiant, as Nate and Angie said their vows of marriage to each other, and their God.

CHAPTER 39
BACK BONE

Robin didn't know exactly how to react when Nathan placed his arm around the woman's shoulder and pulled her close to him. Part of her felt jealousy, but mostly it made her angry. She deeply feared where her inquisition might lead. She was almost sorry she had even asked.

When Nathan walked up to where Angie stood on the cabin porch and put his arm around her shoulder, it was as if he were protecting her. In a way, with people like Robin Gundersen, David Greene, and Keith Weathers in the world, he felt like he needed to.

"Robin, this is my wife. She is my bride," Nathan revealed, but it was almost like time had stood still. She couldn't move, and her breathing was labored almost as if she had just been sucker-punched.

Angie could tell the woman standing in front of them was distressed. "Would you like to sit down?" she offered with the kindness that was natural for her.

Robin, with head down and looking directly at the floorboards of the porch, shook her head in non-acceptance of Angie's invitation.

Nathan felt a twinge of sorrow for her. He never meant to hurt her like this, but it was her fault that she and David even needed to come here. She could have heard about his marriage through the grapevine. Perhaps it would have been a lesser blow to learn about it from a distance.

Robin's attention was drifting from the assignment at hand due to Nathan's revelation of marriage to Angie. How could this possibly have happened without her knowing about it? Was there something she could've done to have stopped it?

Angie clung to Nathan closely as did Sandy behind them. Jasper, who had become Sandy's dog since she and her mother moved into Nathan's cabin, stayed at her side.

"Nathan has told me quite a bit about you, Robin," Angie spoke directly to her. "I know all of this must come as quite a shock to you. Nathan and I only knew each other for three weeks before we were married."

Robin would have considered this a marriage of pity for the woman with the crippled daughter, or maybe even spite directed towards her, if Angie hadn't been so attractive. She could tell why Nathan became smitten by her.

"I must admit, I am surprised to learn you two are married," Robin wasn't telling a lie as she spoke. "I usually make it my business to know what people are up to!"

"Oh, and about that. Mr. Greene, I apologize about the surveillance equipment malfunctioning that you installed in my cabin," Nathan let the cat out of the bag.

Robin couldn't follow Nathan's quip about surveillance equipment, but she was relieved that she didn't know what he was referring to. Glancing over at David, by the look on his face, she sensed he understood completely.

"You can also let Mr. Weathers know I paid him enough money to cover the cost!" he added.

Robin stared at Nathan with contempt for his tone of voice. She detected that David seemed perturbed by Nathan's revelation too. Although it had been several weeks since he had listened in on Nathan's conversations, learning that Keith had indeed been correct about Nathan discovering the equipment, when David had truly hoped it had just been a malfunction, caused his contempt for Nathan Peerless to grow expeditiously.

Feeling disdain for everything that had occurred since they arrived on the cabin porch, David determined it was his time to go on the offensive.

"And this girl, this is your daughter?" David abruptly inquired of Angie.

Nathan stepped between David and Angie, instructing her that she didn't need to answer any of his questions.

"Her name is Sandy, and yes, she's my daughter," Angie answered.

"She's also the reason *you're* here, isn't she, Robin?" he asked in a firm manner.

"Yes, she's the reason," Robin answered, trying to display an innocent look on her face.

David turned the questioning towards the young girl thinking she would be much easier prey than her mother. "And this fraud Healer Boy that married your mother, he's convinced you to play wheelchair bound, and miraculously find healing and voila, now magically you walk?"

"Apparently, you've never been hurled through the windshield of a 2007 Honda Accord, now have you, Mr. Greene? My guess is that you've never had your spine fractured in seven places with the prognosis that you would never walk again, now have you, Mr. Greene?" Sandy prothesized like an experienced trial lawyer.

"Until Nathan healed you?" Robin interrupted.

"Nathan didn't heal me," Sandy proclaimed with a loud voice. "God did!" she declared.

Sandy went on to explain that Nathan had a gift. A powerful gift. A divine gift. With all the wisdom of the ages, she proceeded to speak the truth.

"A gift is a present. Somebody gives you a present to use and enjoy. God has given Nathan this gift to use, and God let me share it. Anybody that would force somebody to sell his gift, or tell him how to use it, well, they're wrong and they're criminals. If you must question whether I'm telling the truth, then I suggest you should have done your research. There is more than enough evidence at Dr. Johnson's office, or the Rehabilitation Hospital in Denver, as to my medical condition. Kinda sloppy of both of you, I think."

Nathan's pride in Sandy and Angie beamed at the wisdom shown by her daughter. Nathan no longer had to fight to defend himself. He had married the woman that God provided for him, and he now had a daughter who would serve God with all the fervor she could muster.

"Ms. Gundersen, my husband promised nothing to me or my child," Angie spoke with conviction. "As my daughter said, he gave us a *gift* and asked nothing in return for it. There was no monetary gain, no entrance fee, only God's love. Perhaps that might have been a lesson God could have better served you with," Angie said, but this time it was a defensive in-your-face tone of voice.

Robin sensed she had met her match. This woman was the 'mountain girl, I'm okay without a dishwasher, don't mess with my man' type of gal that Nathan had always wanted. She really understood him better than Robin could ever have. She walked up to Nathan and gently touched his arm. "Congratulations to both of you, Nathan," Robin softly said. "Sandy, enjoy your newfound life and happiness. Take good care of my dog."

Sandy smiled and retorted, "*My dog!*"

Robin motioned for David Greene to follow her off the porch and they climbed into the SUV with the illegal tinted windows and drove down the gravel road away from the cabin.

David noticed that Robin had a tear in her eye. He would never understand why, so he didn't ask. He did question why she had bailed out on Keith's orders.

"Because Sandy was right. We were sloppy!"

"Keith is sick, isn't he? He needed us to get blackmail material to force Nathan to come and heal him, didn't he?" David inquired.

"No," she replied with a matter-of-fact tone in her voice. "Only God can heal people. I just learned that lesson a little too late."

CHAPTER 40
MEMORIAL

Robin was exhausted when she finally arrived back at her apartment in Nashville. The mental strain of processing everything that had happened on the trip to confront Nathan had overwhelmed her. She left David at the airport in Denver as he said he needed to go to his home in Sarasota first, before returning to Nashville.

She assured him that because she had ended the visit and interrogation with Nathan, she would be the one to call Keith. But first, she needed to sleep.

Looking at the alarm clock on her dresser, she saw that she had only been asleep for a couple of hours when her cell phone rang. The caller ID showed Ron LaGrand.

"Odd for him to be calling me," she thought as she rushed to regain some alertness.

"Robin, this is Ron. Sorry to bother you as I know you've been on a trip, but thought I'd better let you know that Keith is in the hospital. Hospice has been called in. They don't expect him to make it very long."

"Hospice...the hospital?" She had a difficult time absorbing what Ron had just told her.

"If you want to see him, you know, to give him your last respects, then you'd better go now," Ron added.

"But what about the trial he was on? His last visit showed so much improvement," Robin quizzed.

"It was an experimental trial. Science doesn't have all the answers," was all Ron could offer in reply.

Cole Stanton sang several of his hit songs that Keith had written, and Robin gave one of several eulogies at Keith's memorial. She guessed there were at least a thousand people in attendance. Some genuinely sad that the man who made them famous or successful had passed, and some that couldn't wait to prey on his absence to claim his clients.

"What a dirty, dirty business this is," Robin thought to herself. She prided herself on recognizing each and every one of NA's clients and thanking them for coming. She couldn't help but notice that Bobby 'Starkey' Kamp wasn't there. His television series was on hiatus, and she wasn't aware of any other projects that would cause him to miss the memorial of a man that had worked so hard for him.

Nathan sat on his porch throwing a ball out into the yard for Jasper when Angie appeared on the porch. "Keith Weathers passed away. His memorial was today," Angie said without fanfare.

He showed no emotion at the news. All he could think about was the hope that Keith had accepted Christ at the midnight hour.

CHAPTER 41
LAST RIGHTS

He threw his car keys on the table next to the front door and shuffled through his mail. Placing his mail on the table, David felt a lot of apprehension at the death of his boss. For the last several years he had provided a service for Keith that might not be considered very ethical.

He couldn't imagine where his type of service might fit into the hierarchy of Nashville Amusements now. He doubted that the new leadership, whoever that might be, would be willing to go to the depts of deceit that Keith would encourage and allow him to do.

He assumed Robin would become the new CEO, but that information wasn't allowed for someone like him to know. The whiskey bottle sitting on the kitchen countertop suddenly gained an enlightened view in his eyes. Now he wasn't sure just what his future held, and at this moment in time, being alert and able to make quick decisions wasn't important.

Grasping the glass that he had used before from the bottom of the sink, he ran some water into it to give it a rinse. Walking to the freezer he grabbed an ice cube and, with the clink of the ice in the glass, prepared to pour the whiskey over it.

Carrying the drink to the small kitchen table that was just big enough to accommodate two chairs, he sat down and glanced out the lone window at the sun beginning to usher in dusk. Since he had yet to take a drink, aside from being tired from travel to the memorial service, David's senses came to high alert.

His hearing was keen, and he was certain that he heard footsteps behind him. He had yet to remove the harness that carried the 9MM handgun that he always carried from his shoulder. His instincts kicked in and he reached to remove the gun from its holster.

Before he could produce the weapon that was to be used for his defense, a thin stainless-steel wire was quickly thrown over his head and around his neck. His martial arts training kicked in and David did everything he knew to try and gain a position to defend himself and be able to attack.

The assailant was a worthy opponent. David couldn't turn to see what they looked like, but he imagined that it had to be a big man. Losing his footing, he slid to the ground where he sat on his butt with his feet still shuffling to gain a footing.

The struggle was a valiant one, but David could sense that breath and life were creeping away from him. An ironic thought entered his brain as the last conscious thought he would ever have on this earth and that thought was, "She certainly was beautiful. Stupid man, that Nathan Peerless, to have cast her away."

David Greene's muscles relaxed, and his assailant could tell his job had been completed and completed very well. Releasing the wire from around David's neck, he checked for a pulse. There was none.

The assailant lowered David's upper body to the kitchen floor, took out his cellphone and dialed a number. When somebody answered, he spoke quickly and precisely, "It's done."

"Good. He should've known better than to mess with Leonard Pierce. I'll let the family know justice has been served," the voice proclaimed.

A week later, Bobby 'Starky" Kamp signed a lucrative agent contract with The Leonard Pierce Agency.

CHAPTER 42
GOD'S PLAN

Angie stood behind Nathan who was forced to sit down on his sofa in the cabin living room. She lightly clasped the hand that he had brought to his shoulder seeking hers.

"I don't know what to say, Mike," Nathan said with an air of being flabbergasted.

"Then say you'll do it. Say you'll take over the church as pastor," Mike spoke as a man pleading for his life.

Nathan lifted his head up and twisted his neck backwards to be able to look at Angie. Her eyes revealed to him that any decision had to be directed by God. Mike sat eagerly waiting for a response from his friend, fully anticipating that Nathan would accept the offer.

"So, what made you decide to move down the hill and accept lead pastor at a church that is easily five times larger than Evergreen Evangelical?" Nathan questioned with intrigue and seeking guidance on making a decision this life changing.

"Money," Mike innocently answered.

It would be several minutes before Angie, Nathan and Mike would stop laughing. Mike scooted forward in the chair he was sitting in to posture himself before Nathan. "Look,

I've spent a good many years at this church in Evergreen. I have learned to be a proper steward for what God had called me to do at Evergreen. I made the decision to leave for one reason, and one reason only, my dear friend, and that is God told me to."

Nathan pondered with a focused intent what Mike had just said. Sandy had come into the living room escorted by Jasper after having taken him for his daily walk. "Why all the seriousness?" Sandy posed the inquiry to everyone.

Angie let go of Nathan's hand and moved around to stand by her daughter's side. "Well, honey, Mike has just told us that he is leaving Evergreen Evangelical to take a lead pastor's position at a church in Denver."

"Why would you do that?" Sandy asked, looking directly at Mike.

All three adults simultaneously instructed her not to ask, knowing Mike would start them all laughing again. "Mike has offered the lead pastor's position to me," Nathan told Sandy.

"Oh great, that would make me a PK," Sandy responded.

"PK?" Angie asked out of confusion.

"Pastor's kid," Sandy answered in a matter-of-fact way.

Once again, the room erupted in uncontrollable laughter.

Nathan told Mike that his offer was one that he would have to seriously discuss with Angie and Sandy, and most importantly, God.

"Certainly, I wouldn't expect anything less from you. Try and make it a quick decision though, church leadership is excited to have you accept our offer. Many of that leadership was there when that bus crashed many years ago. They know you are a true man of God," Mike offered.

Later that evening, Nathan and Angie sat in bed preparing to go to sleep. They had discussed the situation Mike had presented to Nathan in depth and together they took it to God in prayer. Angie kissed Nathan good night and turned to switch off the light on the nightstand next to her.

She could tell that Nathan was still restless as she felt him toss and turn. When she finally felt him relax, and a light snore emitted from her husband, Angie closed her eyes, hoping that sleep would arrive.

Angie dreamed.

In her dream, she saw fall aspen leaves swirling. She marveled at their colors. Deep reds, yellows and oranges swirled as if a small tornado were carrying them. Her dream revealed that she was standing at the front entrance to Evergreen Evangelical Church greeting people as they entered the foyer that led to the sanctuary.

She marveled at the new parking lot that had been added to accommodate the growth of the church. She believed that an addition to the church building would be the next project because all these people wouldn't be able to fit inside the sanctuary.

Inside she saw her husband. Blue jeans and western style shirt, greeting his flock and accepting hugs of congratulations from them. Congratulations for the joy they were witnessing today because this service was for parents to dedicate their newborns and young children to raising them for the Lord.

Angie leaned down to kiss the newborn she cradled in her arms.

Then that same voice that had spoken to her before, once again called out to her.

"Justin. His name is Justin."

Her eyes flew wide open. She gently shook Nathan until he awoke and, with a groggy reaction, softly spoke to her, "What's the matter?"

She leaned over to touch Nathan's face and responded to his question. "We must accept the offer, my husband. God just revealed his plan for you and me. Plus, Sandy is going to make a wonderful big sister to her little brother!"

Nathan had no words about what his wife had just revealed to him. "You're sure, my love?"

"Yes. I think I've known for a couple of weeks. He will be a boy, and we will name him Justin."

CHAPTER 43
SACKED

Despite getting a pat on the back from Ron LeGrand for the fine job she had done steering Nashville Amusements since Keith's passing, it made it no easier to accept that she had just been canned.

Robin should have anticipated this result. Deep down she sensed that Keith's reasoning for keeping her around and giving her the position in the company had alternative reasons.

She also believed that the Board of Directors had no clue about all that she knew about Nathan Peerless and was disappointed that she didn't pursue additional legal action against him based on the reports about the healing event in Evergreen.

As she packed her personal belongings into a box, she looked down to realize she had worn the black UGH's that Nathan had bought for her. She also still wore the engagement ring he had given her, and never asked to get it back.

What her future may hold, she hadn't a clue. What had plagued her thoughts for many years was the evening she had first seen Nathan Peerless at the revival. As the revival ended, an older stranger came to sit next to her. He inquired what she thought about what she had just heard and seen. She was too preoccupied to pay attention to the man, and then she realized he was gone.

Robin couldn't shake the nagging feeling that this person might not have been just a man. "Sloppy of me, very sloppy," she thought. As she drove out of the parking lot of Nashville Amusements, she picked up her cell phone to do a Google search, *churches near me.*

CHAPTER 44
SEASON

Nathan picked up a beautiful red, orange, and yellow aspen leaf off the floor of the porch of his cabin. He admired its beauty as he turned it over in his hand multiple times. He brought it to his lips to better feel the crispness of its texture. It was nearing the time to crumble into dust. Fall had always been his favorite season and now it had even more meaning.

The four people who God had brought together in love, healing, and strength were like that aspen leaf. They held on to the branch as long as they could, afraid to usher in a new season in their lives only to discover they were the gateway to a beautiful new future.

Jasper looked at Sandy and back to Nathan as if to say, "I am pleased with this arrangement."

Angie put her arms around Nathan and gazed up at his face. Nathan had never bought into the belief that there was a glow about pregnant women. He now realized he was wrong.

He let go of Angie and walked over to put his arm around Sandy, asking, "Okay, PK. What shall we do with the rest of this beautiful day?"

Angie responded first, "Maybe you should lay down and take a nap. You have souls to save tomorrow!"

"Nope," Nathan replied, "Not today, with my favorite women hanging out with me!"

"Don't forget your son," Angie added.

"Daddy?" Sandy asked, then she stopped in her questioning, "I've never asked you if it's okay to call you that."

Her mere mention of this made Nathan cry. "Of course," he said. "I'm your dad now, and in a way, I always have been."

Angie knew now what God meant when the voice said to her '*Heal his heart*'.

"Daddy, can we build a birdhouse today?" Sandy asked.

"Well, sure we can, but why a birdhouse?" Nathan asked.

"Because they'll need one for the winter." Sandy replied as she listened to the sparrow's chirp as they jumped from branch to branch.

EPILOGUE

"Men can be distracted in our walk with the Lord. There is a clear path on which we walk. In the center of the path, there is light. On either side of the path, there is darkness. As we walk, the lure of temptation can cause us to venture off the path and into the darkness," Nathan proclaimed as he held up his old, tattered bible towards heaven. His congregation was entranced by his sermon and his deliverance of God's word.

"This is the word of God. Inside this cover is the divine word of God. Inside this cover are the pages that have God's word written upon them. There was a time in my life when I forgot just how important these words are. Forgetting these words caused me to venture off the path." Nathan looked to the pitched ceiling of the sanctuary in Evergreen Evangelical Church. He stopped speaking for a moment to close his eyes and it was clear that he had tears flowing from them.

Suddenly, laughter from the congregation responding to the *cooing* coming loudly from his son, Justin, interrupted his emotional moment.

Nathan looked down and out into the congregation where Angie was cradling his infant son.

He felt the warmth dwelling deep inside him. He knew this warmth was from the Spirit. That same Spirit that gave him the spiritual gift that he had taken for granted, but would never again. Nathan could see his path in this life, clearly lit, straight down the middle.

www.ingramcontent.com/pod-product-compliance
Lightning Source LLC
Chambersburg PA
CBHW071157260626
47162CB00003B/1079